ANOTHER WORLD

In preparation

A Woman in The Sky

JAMES HANLEY

Another World

HORIZON PRESS
NEW YORK

First published in the United States
1972 by Horizon Press

Copyright © 1972 by James Hanley

Printed in Great Britain by
Redwood Press Limited
Trowbridge, Wiltshire

Library of Congress Catalog Card No. 72-188191

ISBN 0-8180-0613-7

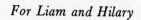

For Liam and Hilary

I

The moment Jones opened the bedroom window he knew it was February. He gave an involuntary shudder and closed his eyes. '*What* a bloody month! Miles long.'

The sea licked the walls, the fog the windows, the house creaked. 'One more long, wide, cold, damp, dark bloody morning,' he thought. He closed the window again and tiptoed quietly across the room, and began to dress. The same as yesterday, and the day before that. One blue shirt, one pair of jeans, an off-white steward's jacket, and the inevitable pair of rope slippers. He then went to the mirror and surveyed himself. A quarter past seven. Damn! And only time to give himself a rub with the flannel. This done, he went over to the bed and stood there quietly contemplating the other occupant. Mrs Gandell was fully stretched, and quietly snoring.

'What a night!'

He crept silently to the door and went out, closing it as silently behind him. He stood for a moment at the top of the staircase, his head a little forward, listening. Complete silence. Save for a tiny glow from a lamp in the dining-room, the Decent Hotel was in utter darkness. Slowly, thoughtfully, he descended the stairs. He opened the front door, and peeped out. No mail. No letters. Perhaps his watch was fast; perhaps *hers* was slow. He strode into the dining-room, inspected the three tables laid for breakfast, examined the contents of the sideboard, wound the clock, and adjusted the transistor. After which he sat down with his head in his hands. Another day. Suddenly he heard a noise from the kitchen, and realised that the maid of all work was doing her duty. Perhaps he had best go along and see.

She was bent over steaming pans when he arrived. He leaned against the door, quietly watching her.

'Morning, Dooley.'

'Morning.'

Dooley, who always placed a premium on words at this time of the morning, now bent lower over her pans, seemed more concentrated on her task. Jones came away from the door.

'Mrs Gandell won't like it, Dooley,' he said, and stepped into the kitchen.

The reply was a bullet. 'Won't like what?' she asked.

'You *know* what,' Jones replied. 'So don't *strain* me.'

She didn't, and went on calmly stirring.

'I had to read her a whole chapter from *The Three Musketeers*,' Jones said.

'At it again,' Dooley replied.

'She still won't like it,' Jones said.

There was no reply. 'Are *you* deaf?' he shouted.

'Were you at it?' asked Dooley, and turned round and studied him. 'She's at it more often than she isn't.'

'A whole hour reading to the bitch,' he said.

Dooley extended her first morning smile. 'Late again,' she said. 'Mrs Gandell's romantic,' she added, and turned to her pans again.

Jones came close behind her. 'What does that mean?' he asked.

'What it says, Jones. And *now*,' her voice climbing, 'and now, will you let me get on with my *work*?'

'She still won't like it,' Jones said.

'What the hell do I care.'

'That's you Irish all over,' he said, 'one boot on and the other off, permanently in transit, so to speak, and accelerating mercilessly.'

'Go to hell.'

Jones didn't, but walked slowly back to the dining-room, and sat down at Mrs Gandell's table. She would soon be down. Thoughts rocked in his head. The night, the reading, the Gandellian moods, the precarious position of the hotel.

'That Prothero chap'll be going today, and after that there'll only be Vaughan. Damn February.'

Suddenly he felt her there, knew her there, and instinctively looked up. And there she was stood at the top of the stairs, and coming slowly down, tall Mrs Gandell, redoubtable Mrs Gandell. Jones often thought of her in purely nautical terms, 'sailing along', and sometimes yawing.

'Are you *there,* Jones?'

Jones jumped to his feet and gave her a mock bow. 'Am here.' And the moment she reached the bottom of the stairs gave forth a blast.

'Aren't I *always* here? Where in hell would you expect me to be?'

'Temper, Jones,' she said, as she came into the dining-room. And the Decent Hotel positively drowned in her first morning smile. No matter from which compass point, Mrs Gandell's approach always placed him in a diminished condition, an eternal reminder to him of her initial observation, when she described him as being 'painfully Welsh, and the height of the chamber pot'. She sailed up to the table, and sat down. Mrs Gandell draped chairs, and never sat comfortably anywhere. Jones leaned across to her.

'Aren't I always here, Mrs Gandell?' he asked.

'Of course you're always here, where else could you *ever* be, Jones, but here,' and she beamed on him, and Jones sat well back in his chair. 'And now,' she said, and sweetly, 'will my grey-haired boy please to bring in the coffee.'

She flung him a cigarette as he got up, and Jones caught it deftly enough, lit it, then rushed off to the kitchen, whilst Mrs Gandell sent smoke clouds ceilingwards.

Like Jones, she too, thought of February, *and* March, *and* April but alas, how heavily they were still anchored in February and its fanged days. She shrugged in sheer disgust. And then Jones arrived with the breakfast.

9

'Jones!'

'Yes, Mrs Gandell?'

She heaved it out, inevitably. 'How I wish the spring would come.'

Jones tittered, then supped noisily at his coffee.

With an almost magisterial solemnity, she said slowly, 'Miss Vaughan had her light on again all night, Jones.'

'Again?' and Jones sat up.

'Sometimes I wonder why I bothered to accept her.'

Jones was at once incisive. 'Because you were *glad* to,' he said. After a short silence she announced that the downstairs closet was blocked again.

'The heavy rains, Mrs Gandell,' he said very casually.

'The rain practically weeps in Wales,' Mrs Gandell said.

'That sounds to me philosophical,' he said, 'and certainly not my way of looking at it,' and Jones supped even more noisily.

'Strange,' she said.

'Search me,' replied Jones.

Silently sipping her coffee, she studied Jones over the rim of her cup. And he in turn studied her, and was fully prepared for the great Gandellian sigh that soon must follow.

'*How* I wish March were here, Jones.' He put down his cup, folded his arms, and sat back.

'Very soon, Mrs Gandell, the lads and lasses from Lancashire will be here, having lifted themselves off their heavy backsides, and made for Wales, of which place they are *very* fond, yes indeed.'

'And the girls with their horrible print dresses,' Mrs Gandell said.

'And the little trout with their mouths wide open, just waiting for the lovely shiny hook, Mrs Gandell,' he cried, sing-song fashion, only to hear her give out another sigh. He leaned to her, stroked her arm, smiled encouragement.

'Soon the wind will lie down, Mrs Gandell, and the ice will *crack*, and the sun will come up. *Lovely*.'

Mrs Gandell surveyed the room, and Jones surveyed Mrs Gandell.

'You won't forget to put a low wattage bulb in Miss Vaughan's room, Jones?' and she resumed sipping her coffee.

'Won't forget,' he replied, his tone of voice both incisive and sepulchral. 'That Pritchard the Stores says daylight is cheapest of all. Sometimes they sit in the dark just to save on the devil's fluid.'

Mrs Gandell groped. 'Devil's fluid?'

'Electric,' Jones said, very curtly.

'Oh!'

'Oh what?'

'Nothing,' she replied and gave him a penetrating look. 'Jones!'

'Yes, Mrs Gandell?'

Suddenly she was peeved. 'Why on earth do you keep on addressing me in that fashion?'

'I do what I want to do, and no more than that,' he replied.

She ran her hand the length of his arm.

'Somehow, I'll never quite understand you, Jones.'

'You may be right,' he said.

He served more coffee, but she waved it away and got up. She rose to her full height, and looked down at her factotum.

'You've checked everything then?'

'I *said* I *had*, Mrs Gandell. Everything is well, and everybody is doing his duty.'

'*Well*?'

Jones was staccato throughout. 'Towel missing number one, broken chamber pot number three, and one hell of a mess in number four. Prothero a little over his time at The Lion.'

'*You* are sometimes over your time at The Lion, Jones.'

'Thank you.'

'There's no need to thank me,' she said.

'I like to do it,' Jones said.

'We must see to the laundry.'

'Will see.'

'I thought I heard that Miss Vaughan crying last night, Jones.'

'*Crying*? Rubbish.'

When she suddenly sat down again, Jones followed.

'I peeped into her room once, Mrs Gandell, and do you know what?'

'What?'

'She was lying flat on her back, staring up at the ceiling. Her arms were folded on her chest, and she was just staring and staring, and smiling . . . .' He paused, then added, 'Just think of that.'

'I hope she didn't see you.'

'Didn't. I think she was well away, Mrs Gandell.'

He was struck by a sudden puzzlement on the Gandellian features.

'Strange,' she said.

Jones stiffened, and almost exploded in her face. 'Strange? Nothing's *strange*, Mrs Gandell. It's the way you look at a thing, that's all.'

'I don't quite follow you.'

'Shouldn't if I were you, Mrs Gandell,' he snapped.

'You are a moody little man, Jones.'

'Thank you.'

'No need to go on thanking me.'

Jones leaned very close across the table. 'What does *that* mean?'

Mrs Gandell spoke so quietly that Jones had to strain to catch the words.

'Perhaps a woman like Miss Vaughan talks in her sleep.'

And Jones shouted, 'Does it matter?'

'What on earth's the matter with you this morning, Jones?'

Jones banged down his cup. '*Nothing*.' And after a pause, 'Why not ask her yourself?'

'I might do that,' she said.

'Do it.'

Her sudden burst of laughter rang out like bells.

'You *are* moody today, Jones.'

He got up, went round to her, bent low, hissed close to her ear.

'I am *not* moody, I am not curious, I am not complaining.'

It startled her. 'Is something wrong, Jones?'

'Nothing is wrong,' and she felt a strong grip on her arm. '*Nothing.*'

Her change of expression astonished him, and he drew away from the table, but she got up and followed him; she took his arm. 'You won't leave me, Jones?'

The reply was quite hollow. 'No,' he said.

'I'm grateful,' and she sighed softly.

'Don't be *too* grateful,' he snapped back.

Suddenly she was stroking his hair. 'I'll remember that,' she said.

'Please yourself.'

He turned his back on her, stared at the hall door, and announced through his teeth that no papers had yet arrived, and no post. 'They'll come,' she said, and offered him a beautiful smile. Their moments had been so absorbing that neither of them had noticed that one of their guests, a Mr Prothero from Melin, had actually come down, and was now seated at his table, the perennial thriller propped up against the sugar basin, his head buried in the text.

'There, Jones,' she cried, and gave him a violent push, suddenly caught his arm and pulled him back. 'I hope you'll remember what I said, Jones,' and all authority lay behind it. Jones nodded, but said nothing. When Mrs Gandell hoped, his claws shone. The loud creak on the stairs made them both look up. Miss Vaughan was just coming down. 'Hurry, Jones.'

Jones wanted to shout 'Good morning,' but changed his

mind, and grabbing a napkin he rushed off to attend to Mr Prothero. He hovered over the traveller in plastics.

'Morning, Mr Prothero.'

'Morning,' growled Prothero, never taking his eyes off the thriller. 'No bloody papers, yet,' he said. 'And no post either.'

Jones, still hovering, began to knead his hands. 'Will come, sir.'

'And how about some service,' shouted Prothero, 'I mean service.'

'Yes sir,' and he immediately rushed off to the kitchen, to appear a few seconds later bearing a tray that he placed on the sideboard.

'Looks like my bloody breakfast at last,' Prothero said.

'*Is*,' replied Jones, and served him. A mixture of Quilp and Heep, he served him smilingly. 'And Mr Prothero is leaving us today then. Well well!'

He stood back, still kneading his hands.

'I am.'

'Then you will enjoy your parting cup of tea, I'm sure, sir. Will bring luggage down, Mr Prothero, sir,' extending an oily smile. 'Yes indeed.' He rubbed the palms of his hands together, and whenever Jones did this, his fingers tapered in the air.

Miss Vaughan cried from her table. 'Mr Jones?'

'Coming ... *com* ....', and he hurried to her table, bowed, gave her his morning smile, 'Yes, Miss Vaughan?'

'*Breakfast*, Mr Jones,' Miss Vaughan said.

She sometimes addressed him as Mr Jones, and he loved that. He began serving her.

'I hope you have slept well, Miss?'

She looked up over her spectacles, and quietly replied that she had indeed.

'Good. Good.'

Miss Vaughan always sat well back in her chair when Jones served meals, disliking a certain closeness about him, his rubbing of palms and kneading of fingers, his oily smile, and often idiotic grins. Suddenly he was too close to her ear.

'Same as usual, I'm afraid, Miss Vaughan, and I'm even more afraid that it's cod again in the evening. With a little colouring of course.'

'Where is Mrs Gandell?'

'Just left the office, dear,' replied Jones.

Miss Vaughan adjusted her spectacles, and said severely, 'I am not your dear, Mr Jones.'

Jones grinned, drew back. 'No indeed, Miss, you are not. Did you wish to speak with Mrs Gandell? Pity you missed her. She's in the kitchen at the moment.'

'Later then,' and Miss Vaughan began her breakfast.

Jones stood respectfully behind her. He thought she ate her food quite daintily.

'Mrs Gandell has gone off to do her duty, Miss Vaughan,' he said. 'And as usual,' he continued, 'with sails aloft, and a fine wind blowing, and I call that optimism with a star at its head, Miss.' He bent lower, closer still, and in conspiratorial whispers went on. 'She is always doing her duty, in the rooms and out of the rooms, counting the half-pence in the basement, counting the crumbs that are left, and watching and listening, and watching those that watch, and listening again, and wondering, and hoping *all* the time. Think of that, Miss Vaughan. Ah! Poor Mrs Gandell! How she feels the weight of the world on her back, yes indeed, and what a weight it is, but I expect you know that, dear.'

Miss Vaughan frowned, and Jones cringed. '*So* sorry,' he said. 'But Iesu mawr! She is as sharp as a razor blade, Miss Vaughan, and cuts time to shreds.'

Suddenly there was a loud thud in the hall, followed by Prothero roaring, 'Papers, Jones,' and he rushed off to collect them, and the mail. He handed one to Prothero, saying, 'And no mail again for Mr Prothero. Dear dear!'

Prothero immediately vanished behind the spread pages, though not before calling across the room, 'And how is Miss Vaughan today?'

'Quite well, thank you,' Miss Vaughan replied, and

15

nibbled her toast.

Prothero's head appeared over the paper.

'I've an uncle over at Derwen that's almost *too* well,' and with a loud chortle vanished behind the paper.

'More toast, Mr Jones.'

'Certainly Miss Vaughan.'

Jones preened, and Jones was fulsome.

'Thank you.'

'Will there be anything else, Miss?'

'Nothing really,' and Miss Vaughan gave him her first smile of the day.

He grinned from ear to ear. 'There should always be something,' he said. 'Tell me, do you like your room?'

'It is very nice,' she replied, paused, then asked, 'and you, Mr Jones, you like being here?'

Jones came erect, threw out his chest, clapped hands.

'Like it? *Me*? I just love that, Miss Vaughan. Course I do. I'm the fish-flesh man that likes everything,' and slowly rocked on his heels.

'Sometimes, Mr Jones, you are very funny.'

Miss Vaughan began folding her napkin.

'You astound me, Miss. *Why,* everything's funny. Didn't you know that?'

'You may be right.'

'I am. And how is Miss Vaughan liking Garthmeilo?'

'It's all right.'

'Good. Good.'

'Thank you.'

'And everything as you wish, I hope,' Jones said.

'Not *too* close, please,' Miss Vaughan said, preparing to rise, and Jones drew back.

'I did hear,' he began slowly, groping, 'I did hear that you came from a place called Melin. I remember Melin myself, especially that row of six cottages beside the post office, always looked like a row of badger's teeth to me,' and the Decent Hotel echoed with Jones's first outright laugh of the day.

He watched her examine minutely the entire contents of her handbag, and later a leisurely powdering of her nose. Abruptly she said, between dabs, 'I hope Mrs Gandell will . . .' but Jones cut in.

'She will,' he said, grinning.

'You don't even know what I was going to say, Mr Jones,' and Miss Vaughan closed her handbag and slowly dusted herself down.

'What I don't know, Miss Vaughan, always excites me more than what I do. Yes indeed.'

Miss Vaughan pushed in her chair, then walked slowly towards the hall.

'Off into the great big world,' he said, following slowly after.

Miss Vaughan stopped dead, turned, and glared at Jones. 'What world?'

Jones didn't know, but he rushed forward and opened the door for her. He banged it loudly behind her.

'Jones!'

When the call came he jumped, swung round, and there was Mrs Gandell sailing across the room.

'Get Mr Prothero's luggage,' she said, and rushed off to her little office, tapping Prothero as she passed. 'Come along, Mr Prothero,' and he followed her in.

'Are you getting that luggage, Jones?'

'Am getting.'

Prothero was waiting for Jones when he came down. He gave Jones a shilling, and he promptly spat on it, and put it in his pocket. 'Thank you, Mr Prothero, sir, thank you.'

Prothero only looked disgusted as he shot out of the hotel.

'Do *hurry,* Jones.'

'Coming, Mrs Gandell,' and when he reached the table discovered that she had already begun her breakfast.

'Ah!' he sighed, sat down, and began his own.

'Only Vaughan left now,' Mrs Gandell said, between sips.

'Indeed! Is that news?'

'I've been thinking,' she went on, suddenly paused, 'yes, I have,' tentatively, carefully watching her factotum. 'I've been thinking it best to –' when Jones cut in.

'Indeed,' he said, huffily. 'What about?'

'There's something I'm not quite certain about this morning.'

Jones dropped knife and fork. 'Oh yes!'

Staring at Jones, she was suddenly conscious of a certain disgust rising in her. Jones was now head down, wolfing his breakfast.

'It could be confusing,' he snapped, and did not look up.

She stabbed it out. 'I *was* saying something, Jones.'

'I gathered that,' and he went on with his breakfast.

Mrs Gandell sipped again. 'You were late again last night, Jones.'

Jones jumped up, gave a short mock bow, and said, '*Sorry.*'

'You said that last time.'

He was on his feet in a flash. 'And I'm saying it *this* time. God Almighty! I only ever go as far as The Lion. And *why*? Tell you. Because beyond it is just a desert. And you never saw such a collection of bent bones as sits in that pub, some of them almost figures of eight from rheumatics.' He paused, his fork in the air. 'I suppose it helps them to lighten an ache in the bone.' There was another pause, he dropped his fork. 'I do my duty, don't I?'

'Of course you do, Jones.'

'Well then,' he shouted.

'Con*trol* yourself.'

Angry bursts from Jones often intrigued and frightened her.

'I thought you liked reading to me, Jones,' she said, and sighed.

'That stuff.'

'That *stuff*,' Mrs Gandell said.

'God!' And Jones clapped hands to his head, and rocked

it. He looked at her through spread fingers. 'And after I've reached the last page?' he said.

Her mood changed, she smiled. 'You always think of something, Jones.'

'I'm sick of reading,' he said.

She gave him the sweetest smile. 'Jones?'

'Well?'

'There was something I wished to ask.'

'*Ask.*'

'I hope you don't make a habit of visiting Miss Vaughan's room.'

'Don't you? You go into all the rooms when they're out, seen you.'

'Are you spying on me, Jones?'

He gave a final noisy sup at his coffee and sat back. 'I happen to be where I am at the time, Mrs Gandell, and nowhere else.'

She threw him a cigarette, and lit one herself. 'Whatever I may think about you, Jones, I shall always remember that you are good to me.'

'Thank you.'

'There's no need to go on thanking me all the time.'

'I do what I wish to do.'

She avoided his glance, and stared windowards, and he knew she was still thinking of that too long month.

'Thinking of winter again?'

'I always think of it.'

He gripped the table, leaned across, and said, 'You're always thinking of it, Mrs Gandell. Got it on the brain.'

It upset him when she roared with laughter.

He leaned closer still. 'What do *you* know about winter? You know nothing, I mean nothing. There are winters in Wales that are longer than the Stations of the Cross. When I was a child I practically *ate* winter, in my bed, and in my school, and in my chapel, and in my head, and on any bloody road I happened to be.'

There was a momentary silence, and then she said very

quietly, 'Jones, one of these days you will be outgrown by your own tensity.'

He growled at her. 'Ah . . .'

'I was . . .'

'Well?' he snapped.

She dismissed him with a wave of the hand. 'Another time,' she said.

'Never strangle your thoughts, Mrs Gandell. *Say* it.'

He stood up, leaned over her, and said quietly, 'What is the matter?'

'The hotel is not paying.'

'It will.'

'I rather doubt that, Jones.'

'I said it will.'

The optimism made her smile, and Jones didn't like it very much.

'All the same,' she began . . . when he cut in again.

'Your – I mean, you won't leave here, Mrs Gandell?'

'I have been thinking about it, Jones.'

He slumped in the chair. 'You can't leave me? Leave here?' and he got up and rushed to the hall, where he stood staring at the wall. She followed him.

'You're not upset, are you, Jones?'

She put a hand on his shoulder, but he remained motionless. '*Jones.*'

He swung round. 'You can't. You can't leave me, *here.*'

She turned him slowly round, smiled. 'What a strange little monkey it is that lives so near to me, and has been so good to me all this time. Come along, Jones. Head up,' and she put a hand under his chin. 'You have always been loyal, Jones, always.'

He hated her when she patted his head, but she patted it now. 'There, there!'

He gripped her arms, stuttered, 'You won't go, Mrs Gandell?'

'I - - -'

His grip tightened. 'I said you won't *go*, leave me. *Here.*'

'I was only thinking about it, Jones. No more than that,' and she turned her back on him and went back to her table. Jones did not move. She lit another cigarette. 'Come here, Jones.'

He came, stood intently watching her, then sat down.

'More coffee,' she said, jug in air.

'*No.*'

'Manners, Jones,' she shouted in his face, 'I said *manners.*'

'Ah . . . .'

She flung him yet another cigarette. 'There's work to be done.'

'I'm not blind, I'm not deaf, Mrs Gandell,' he replied.

The silence seemed too long, the torrent too surprising. Jones was on his feet again, half way across the table, glaring down.

'Only one thing lower than low, Mrs Gandell, one thing worse than worse and that's if Jonesy here suddenly took it into his head to *depart,* yes, and walked right out of this place. Tell you what would happen, you great fat bitch, tell you. You'd *die.* Yes, and all that would be left for you is Vaughan, the upstairs angel, with her silly bloody dreams about princes and stars and seas, and her dead grandmother, and the shadow on her wall. Perhaps in her Vaughan way she might help you, as a creature, yes indeed.'

She pushed him away. 'What on earth are you talking about, Jones?'

'You know what I'm talking about,' he replied, 'you do . . . know.'

'Know *what?*' and she too, was on her feet, and the thunder a little too close to the Jones ear.

When he looked at her again, it was with a certain disgust. 'When you *shout,* Mrs Gandell, I think only of the world's bosun.'

She gripped and shook him. 'And you, when you have your bloody moods, are the world's *bugger.*'

'Thank you,' he said, and sat down.

'Why are we doing this?'

'Why are we?'

And they both sat down. Jones picked up his empty coffee cup, and put it to his lips, and appeared to be drinking copiously. Mrs Gandell bowed her head, traced patterns with her finger among the bread crumbs. When she looked up Jones was sitting with his back to her.

'Jones?'

He swung round. 'Yes, Mrs Gandell?'

'I've been thinking of letting Miss Vaughan have the larger room now that Mr Prothero has gone.'

'Indeed!'

'Yes.'

'She likes where she is.'

'I'll talk to her about it.'

'*I* said, she won't *like* it.'

'She doesn't appear to go out very often, Jones.'

'Does she *have* to go out then?'

'All right, all right. No need to get excited about it.'

'I never get excited, Mrs Gandell,' he said.

'Then get excited,' she said, and swept out of the dining-room.

'Come along. Laundry.'

'Oh yes,' Jones said, stumbling after.

At the top of the stairs he turned and faced her.

'Tell you something, Mrs Gandell. If you left me, left this place, you'd always be sorry about it. I was anchored in this town long before you arrived from that un-nameable place of yours in Yorkshire, and I've been here so long that you'll find my shoulder rubs over half the town. My heels were dug in the ground long before you ever smelt Wales. This hotel depends as much on me as on you. I am a person that is always thoughtful about his condition, I know where I am, and I know where my place is, and my motto has always been, cling, clutch. It's the way it goes, you see.'

She gave him a violent push and he landed up outside

the door of the linen room. 'There's work to do,' she said. 'And no one is indispensable,' she added, and bent over the laundry basket.

'Have you met the man with the chariot in his head, Mrs Gandell?'

'The man with the chariot in his head?'

'Minister Thomas,' he said. 'Lives with his sister at Ty Newdd. Now there's a piece of grey granite, Mrs Gandell, if ever there was. She's ten years younger than him and acts as his housekeeper. *He* practically lives in his little study, always reading, and writing. Lives in a big black chair with a high back to it, *very* small his study is, and the walls are damp.'

'All the walls in Wales are damp,' she said, and flung him a towel.

'There's lots of spiders in his study, too, Mrs Gandell. Very nice, very cosy. Yes indeed. Met him in the street the other afternoon, and what d'you think he said to me?'

'What?'

' "Jones," he said, "I think you have a very common mind".'

Jones tittered, and Mrs Gandell finally closed down the basket.

'I gave him *such* a freezing look, Mrs Gandell, and I said to him, "Mr Thomas, I love my common mind." He walked away then with his head well in the air, and his mouth was as tight shut as any old purse that's got nothing in it.'

'I think I've seen him passing through the town.'

Jones sat on the laundry basket and swung his legs.

'Is that all, Jones?'

'All.'

'Good.'

He gave her a smile and said, '*How* good?'

'Too early for riddles, Jones,' and she gave a curious little laugh. She lit a cigarette, and she didn't offer him one.

'D'you remember last year, Mrs Gandell, when we had

those two queer guests from a place called Padiham, some-where in Lancashire, I think. Very queer lot indeed.'

'What about them?'

'*What* about them? God Almighty! You're not actually going to tell me that you remember them, you've never been very good at remembering, since you like forgetting best of all. But *I* remember them. Smelt of many a Lanca-shire alley, yes indeed. A pair of queer fish, Mrs Gandell,' he followed this with a positive sneer. 'And you were so kind to the bastards, weren't you? *Such* an obliging week that was,' and she felt his breath against her ear, and at the same moment the grip of his fist. 'Yes, and at the end of that lovely, golden week, and only a single trout between them, they went off, and after that their cheques *bounced,* Mrs Gandell. Remember? I do. Can you recall?'

Her expression was one of utter bewilderment; she could only stare at Jones. '*Well?*'

Jones continued, his tone of voice changed in a moment, and he said excitedly, 'No. You don't remember because you don't *want* to. You remember nothing if you don't want to, Mrs Gandell. But I remember everything. Sur-prised you don't. It *was* an occasion,' and he drew away from her, almost in disgust, his tone scathing. 'You don't want to remember because you weren't even around, so to speak, no, because you were flat on your back with your hands to your eyes that couldn't quite close from the sheer surprise of it. Surprise had a nice curl in its tail that morn-ing. And where was Jonesy? I'll tell you. Jonesy was in his place, doing his duty, and so he crawled off to the bank with a fistful of the most beautiful excuses any Welsh bank manager was ever offered. The balm on my tongue *then,* Mrs Gandell. And do you know *what?* He gave your over-draft a lovely nudge, you know all about that weird red line that sometimes sails into the black ones. Yes. So a week that started with teeth in it actually closed with velvet. But only because I was here, Jonesy of the Decent Hotel was behind you again, your handmaid and helpmate, and shuffler and scuffler was propping you up, that works so hard to keep the ragged and tottering ends of your hotel together. I never even asked you to say thank you. Why? Because I'm decent, Mrs Gandell. Decent.'

She drew away from him, and from the tense moment.

'So you won't just pack up and go, Mrs Gandell, will you? You wouldn't leave Jonesy here, stuck, battered, buggered, finished?'

'You *really* are funny, Jones,' she said, and went up and hugged him.

'Thank you,' he said, and hugged her, too.

'And we can't stay here half the morning, either,' she said, and pulled him off the basket, pushed him towards the door, and opening it, kicked him out.

'I shall aways be the odd curve in your designs, Mrs Gandell.'

They went slowly downstairs, hand in hand.

'Ah! Come the spring,' she sighed.

'They'll come rolling along, I'm sure, Mrs Gandell, and Jonesy will be pleased, because what pleases you pleases me. So you won't just *go,* will you, Mrs Gandell?'

'I'll think about it,' she said.

She felt his hand again, as he said, 'If I wasn't ordinary, Mrs Gandell, I wouldn't know what to do. Fact. I knew you were sad this morning, knew it as soon as I got up, but you're not sad now, are you?'

She shook her head. 'No, Jones, I am not.'

'Thank you,' he said, and gave her a Jonesian bow. It made her laugh.

'You'll have to turn to in the kitchen, Jones, at least until I get somebody else.'

'Will do.'

'Get along,' and she pushed him ahead of her towards the tiny office. She sat down, and pored over her ledger, whilst Jones, as was his wont, went to the wall, and leaned there, his legs crossed, watching her. She took an envelope from a pigeon hole and handed it to him. 'Here are Dooley's card and wages,' she said. 'Give them to her, and remember I do not wish to see her. And see that she leaves by the back door.'

'Yes, Mrs Gandell.'

'And whilst you're there, make a pot of tea, and bring it here.'

'Yes, Mrs Gandell.'

He fingered the envelope. 'Pity,' he said.

'Pity *what*?'

'Nothing,' Jones replied, speaking from boot level.

'Remember what I said.'

'Will say.'

'Then *go*.'

'Am gone.'

She checked figures, names, she bent low over the ledger, the real Bible of the Decent Hotel. She erased, she added, subtracted. Suddenly she closed the book, and sat back in her chair. She was feeling both sorry and glad. Glad that Dooley was gone, a useless hussy. She closed eyes, became reflective, talked to herself, thought of her one remaining guest. Quiet Miss Vaughan, withdrawn Miss Vaughan. Arriving so suddenly from nowhere, anywhere. So simple in her contents, so obliging, so satisfied, and scarcely any trouble at all. Only God Himself could have guided such a one to the Decent Hotel in its longest dragging month. She had asked Jones where she came from, and Jones said that he never asked anyone where they came from, and that seemed that. She smiled suddenly, remembering his description of the Vaughan room. 'You could write the Litany of the word One on her door, Mrs Gandell. Yes indeed, a *very* small room, and so *tight*, Mrs Gandell.'

'Box room, Jones,' she had replied.

She remembered the sing-song narration, that brought out a certain soft yell in the Jones voice. 'One bed, one chair, one dressing-table, one looking-glass, one *hair*brush, one comb, one jar of cream, one dress hanging behind a door, one tube of something, squeezed it, Mrs Gandell, kind of miraculous mud perhaps, you'd *know,* one carpet, one shelf and some books on it.'

The sound of raised voices, followed by that of a loudly banging door, told her that Dooley had finally gone.

She closed her eyes against the morning, against the rain, the darkness; she thought of the sun. When she opened them again Jones was there, just inside the little glass door, the tray in his hand. She immediately closed the ledger. 'There you are.'

'And here I am, Mrs Gandell. See you've been at it again.'

'I am always *at* it, Jones.'

'Yes, Mrs Gandell.'

'And I've been thinking that in some ways we are lucky.'

'Indeed.' Jones leaned against the wall, slowly supped the tea.

'I am more cautious than you,' he concluded, 'I can only say *perhaps.*'

She flung him the reply. 'And I say we are, that's all.'

He came over, put down the cup, leaned close.

'One should never be too certain about anything, Mrs Gandell. No indeed for there's a mixture of strange cunning and wisdom in most things. Have you ever noticed how the wise ones answer the questions too soon, and the cunning ones too late. Perhaps you haven't,' and he dragged the remainder of his sentence. 'Perhaps you never will.'

She got up, pushed past him and went to the window.

'Still raining.'

'That will be a very *real* fact, later, as big as a fist. I have to go out in it. The gin's run out.'

'And the cigarettes,' she said. She could only think of gin and cigarettes as lifebelts in this dreary month.

'The Lion will be closed,' he said.

'The Lion has a back *door,* Jones.'

She came away from the window, put a hand on his shoulder. 'Try not to overdo it, Jones, since I am not an entirely stupid woman, so that I could sometimes wish that you were not so self-conscious about conveying to me that you are *always* doing your duty.'

'Thank you.'

An instantaneous smile lit her face, and it puzzled Jones. 'Oh yes?' he said.

'I was only thinking of your Minister Thomas,' she said, and gave a tiny little laugh.

It upset Jones. 'And what are you laughing about, Mrs Gandell? Because he's Welsh, because he's chained to the cross, because he's craggy and fifty, and washes his feet every week. Or because he has the big ache and the ice in his prayers? Well then?'

'He's less funny than you, Jones.'

'Does he *pay* for calling? Perhaps some crumbs are better than no crumbs.'

'There,' she exclaimed, and slapped his face.

He grinned in her face and again said, 'Thank you, Mrs Gandell.'

'You'd better get off, hadn't you, Jones?'

And she followed him to the stairs, and stood there watching him go up. When he reached the top he turned and offered her a smile. 'What a mixture,' she thought.

She stood there, waiting for him to appear, which he did, wearing an old raincoat. He carried an umbrella, but no hat.

'Good.'

They stood close together in the hall. 'You won't be long?'

'I won't be long,' he replied, and opened the front door. Rain came in, and he stood back, fingering the umbrella.

'Not inside the house, Jones, I'm tired of telling you that.'

He stood down on the step, looked up, surveyed the sky.

'The clouds have very wet faces,' he said, 'and right down there the sea is fast asleep. Ah!' and he waved the opened umbrella. 'I really don't like the sea when the wind's lying flat atop of it, no indeed. And such a *queer* sort of light seems to come over the place.'

'Get along, Jones,' and gave him a push.

He turned to her and said quietly, 'One of these days you may push Jonesy just too much. Remember that, Mrs Gandell, won't you.'

'Get along,' and she banged the door furiously behind him, and went and sat at one of the dining-room tables. She was aware of the draughts in the room. She would have to do something about it. She went to the office and sat down, then immediately got up again and went upstairs. She sat down on the bed.

'If I can get through the month,' she thought, 'yes, if I can get through the month.' She went to the black corner cupboard and opened it. The empty gin bottles seemed a direct affront, and she hoped her factotum wouldn't be too long. The cigarette burned away in her fingers, and she reached for another. The packet was empty. 'Damn!'

In the nine months she had been proprietress of the Decent Hotel, she had only been into the town on three occasions, from each of which journeys she had returned feeling like something of a ghost in the place. It made her realise how English she was, how Welsh *they* were. Sometimes she asked herself why she had ever left Yorkshire. She heard a key turn in the lock. 'It must be Jones,' and rushed from the room. Half way downstairs the door opened, and there was Miss Vaughan coming into the hall.

'Why, Miss Vaughan? Is something wrong?' and she hurried to her. 'My dear!' she exclaimed, noting the pallor, 'Is anything the matter?'

She fussed her all the way to a table and sat down, 'Are you ill, my dear?'

'I'd an awful headache, and Mr Blair said I could go home.'

'I'm sorry, dear,' and she rushed off to the kitchen, returning quickly with a glass of water and two aspirins. 'There now! Take those. You'll be all right. And after that

29

I should rest in your room.'

'Thank you, Mrs Gandell,' and she swallowed the tablets and finished off the water. 'Sorry to be a bother.'

'You are no bother at all.'

'I'll go up now.'

'Of *course*,' and she came closer to her one remaining guest, and added, 'I *do* hope you'll be better by lunch time.'

Miss Vaughan stared, and didn't seem to know the answer to that. She rose, and Mrs Gandell said abruptly, 'Of course now that Mr Prothero has gone, I could let you have his room, it is larger than your own.'

It produced the faintest smile from Miss Vaughan. 'Thank you, but I'm quite all right where I am, Mrs Gandell. I like my room, and do not wish to change it.'

'I'm glad to know that,' said Mrs Gandell, and longed for a cigarette.

'And thanks for the aspirins.'

'Tut! Tut! Nothing at all, my dear. I thought you would have liked a larger room.'

'I would not have liked a larger room,' said Miss Vaughan, and gathered up her things.

'I . . . see.'

'I'm glad of that. There are some people, Mrs Gandell, that simply do *not* see.'

'Yes . . . all right now?'

'I'm better now, thank you.'

'I was wondering if you'd like to dine at my table this evening, Miss Vaughan?'

'I'd rather not.'

'As you wish.'

Miss Vaughan said thank you again, and stressed it. 'You do not yourself go into the town very often, Mrs Gandell.'

Mrs Gandell was too surprised to answer.

'Perhaps you do not like Garthmeilo?'

'I don't always want to go, and often I need not.'

'Of course. Jones is a most helpful man.'

'Most helpful, Miss Vaughan.'

'How nice.'

'Strange, but I feel rather worried today, Miss Vaughan,' and the moment she said it, she regretted it.

'People that worry are silly. Mr Prothero did not stay long.'

'I hope he'll return soon,' replied Mrs Gandell.

'I can see you are sorry he's gone. People are like that. They just *go*.'

And Mrs Gandell stuttered back, 'Yes . . . of course.'

'You don't feel at all lonely here, Miss Vaughan?'

On which Miss Vaughan sat down again, took off her spectacles, and slowly began to clean them. 'What a question to ask, Mrs Gandell,' she said, 'as if it mattered.'

'I mean . . . well, you are Welsh, that I know, I suppose you have your people, your father for instance . . . .'

Miss Vaughan looked up, frowned. 'My father is *not*,' she said.

'How awful!'

'He went over a cliff at Tenby, Mrs Gandell.'

'I *am* sorry,' but Miss Vaughan's sudden laugh quite shocked her.

Miss Vaughan picked up her things, and got up, and as she moved away, said quietly, 'Do you believe in what you have, Mrs Gandell?' She moved towards the stairs, a bewildered Mrs Gandell at her side.

'Believe in what I have?'

'I never question anything that I have, Mrs Gandell, and I cling to it.'

'Yes, yes, of course, I do understand,' and Mrs Gandell again dived into her pocket for the cigarette that wasn't there.

'Once, I really thought I wanted certain things myself, Mrs Gandell, but I thought hard about it, and after a while I knew I didn't want them, and I forgot them at once.'

'I *see*,' not seeing.

'And now I'm going to my room.'

'I hope you'll be yourself by lunchtime, Miss Vaughan,' but Miss Vaughan made no comment, and went on up. Mrs Gandell remained rooted where she stood, still staring up after the departed guest. 'How odd,' she thought, but the practical side of her spoke with a greater resolution. 'She pays regularly, is little inconvenience here, and interferes with nobody.'

She longed for a cigarette, for a straight gin; if Miss Vaughan was odd, so too, had been the morning, and she went and sat at her table in the dining-room, and patiently waited for the return of Jones.

2

Miss Vaughan often talked to Miss Vaughan, and did so now, as slowly, very slowly, she mounted the stairs to her spartan room. 'It was kind of Mr Blair to let me come home. Such a nice man, so understanding,' and in a flash she was back in the office listening to the orders from him, and from his junior partner, Mr Wilkins, and to the occasional giggling amongst the girls in the outer office. It was the world being attended to, no waiting allowed.

'Bring me those papers at once, Miss Vaughan.'

'Yes, sir.'

'And type this, that, and the other,' cried Mr Wilkins, glaring at her over his spectacles.

'Yes, sir.'

'And please remove this.'

'Of course, sir.'

'And now run along. I will ring when I want you.'

But Miss Vaughan never ran anywhere, but proceeded slowly to her desk, and waited, and listened to the whispers in the outer office. She waited patiently for the spur of the moment, the call to duty.

'Are you *there*, Miss Vaughan?'

A rare occasion when she is not, for she seems to be ceaselessly coming and going, and is always calm, and controlled, and dedicated. She rises and falls upon the turbulent waves of the world, and is unharmed, because one Miss Vaughan hides within the other. On Vaughan ground there were no trespassers, and no road, no bridge, no secret passage and no key to that inner Miss Vaughan that lived so warm and comfortable and sustained by that Miss Vaughan of the office, who was always *there*, the moment she was wanted.

She reached the top stair, touched the doorknob of her room, and gave a little sigh, for this was her moment, coming home, closing the door behind her, shutting out the world. She removed her hat, coat, gloves, and spectacles, and then sat down on her polar bed. 'Ah!' She crossed to the dressing-table, and sat in front of the looking-glass. When she looked in, another Miss Vaughan looked out.

'People *never* stop talking.'

She leaned in closer, her fingertips making a slow voyage over the anatomy of her face.

'I'm glad I'm back.'

She always was. She got up and went and lay on her bed, and switched off the light. Hands behind her head, she stared up at the ceiling. Darkness is kind, and kindest to Miss Vaughan. The silence was so calm, so warm, it hushed her down to a peace. She thought of an October afternoon, an entrance.

She had arrived at Garthmeilo as quietly as a mouse. Only the single porter at the station had witnessed it. She stood motionless on the platform, looking up and down, very aware of his presence, and of the knife-like wind that blew in their faces. And after a while it had seemed to occur to him that somebody *had* actually arrived. He jumped down on the line, and crossed over.

'Can I help you, Miss?' and bent down for her suitcase.

'This is Garthmeilo?'

'That's it. Where were you for?'

'The Decent Hotel.'

'*That* place!'

'That *place*.'

'Then right-ho, and allow me,' and again he reached for her suitcase.

'I will not allow you,' she said, and picked it up, and moved off down the platform.

'You know where it is then?' he called after her.

She stopped, turned, and waited till he came up. 'I shall find it.'

'As you wish,' and the wintry platform echoed with the porter's outright laugh, as he hurried back to the tiny grate in his room to wait for the next train. And Miss Vaughan had stalked out of the station with a firm resolve, the porter's raucous laugh still echoing in her ears. She battled against the wind through every street and alley, and it was black dark when she finally arrived at the hotel. She had walked into the hall, rung the bell, and waited. Mrs Gandell had come bouncing forward, feeling a great relief at the arrival of a new guest. It seemed so splendid that a miracle like this should happen in the middle of a harsh winter. She had carried an extra chair into the tiny office, on which Miss Vaughan sat down, clasped hands, and studied her landlady. Mrs Gandell had never quite forgotten the interview, and not least its brevity, but Miss Vaughan had long forgotten it.

'Miss Vaughan?'

'I am Miss Vaughan.'

'Just a few particulars,' Mrs Gandell had begun, 'you are from . . .'

'I do not think that is very important, Mrs Gandell,' and Miss Vaughan had bent low and peered at the proprietress through her spectacles. 'It *is* Mrs Gandell?'

Mrs Gandell had said that was correct, and had smiled sweetly.

'What will you do in Garthmeilo, Miss Vaughan, if I may ask.'

'You may not ask. It is my business.'

'Of course, of course,' replied Mrs Gandell, and thought quickly, 'Not too much fuss, no indeed.'

Miss Vaughan delved into her handbag. 'I have your terms here, Mrs Gandell. I shall pay you one month in advance,' on which Mrs Gandell positively beamed, and sighed her thanks.

'Please show me to my room.'

'Of course, my dear.'

The notes had never felt warmer in Mrs Gandell's hands,

and she fussed Miss Vaughan all the way up to her attic room.

'There!'

Miss Vaughan looked round, then said quietly. 'It will do. Thank you.'

Mrs Gandell had rushed away very excitedly to make a nice hot cup of tea.

Miss Vaughan opened her eyes, and closed them again.

'It is quiet here, and I am myself,' and she smiled and raised her arms above her head, and stared at her outspread fingers. Sometimes Miss Vaughan thinks of her home, that white cottage far away that seemed always to be lost in the bracken, and sees quite clearly the belt of kingly oaks that stood in the corner of a far field. Sometimes there would come to her ear the distant cold bark of a dog fox, and it made her remember where the blood pulled, and the root held. She remembers the very look and feel and touch and shape of her home, through the windows of which she had often stared with the large, questioning eyes of childhood. She remembers her mother. But now the cottage is leagues away, and life ends up in this small room. Within the area of the kingly oaks life had seemed to rise up, vaunting, but here, in a dark room, it was different. Life crouched. Suddenly she sat up in her bed, and switched on the light. She thought of a coming visit to the dining-room for lunch, and the sight of a tall woman, and a medium-heighted and inexplicable man that answered to the name of Jones.

'I'll go out to lunch,' she thought. 'I'll go out to lunch,' she said.

Her daily journeys from room to office and back again were always voyages. Sometimes she slept like a child, dreamed like a child. But the clock will strike when it must, and another day will break, and she will walk into the world again. Down the same streets, and past the same hurrying and scurrying people that did not seem to matter. The same stride, and the same onward glance, and always the head lifted high, as if it were seeking some new level of air itself. In the hooded darkness that fell the moment she switched off the light, Miss Vaughan again talked to Miss Vaughan.

'A very strange dream I had last night, and when I woke up whole mountains of leaves were fluttering down.' If Miss Vaughan got lost, Garthmeilo always knew where to find her, but did not bother, since one and then another had assumed that she was best lost. Sometimes she walked down to the shore and sat, and watched, and listened, and once watched a moon fall to the sea, heard waves break and die on a long, curling sweep of sand. And once she heard quite distantly the cries of running-by and running-after children, all shrill and winter wild as their energy pounded the shore, but not once had she seen them. And there was the long, lone walk back to her room that was not lonely, and that steady climb away from the tight and noisy streets. Sometimes when the town was very silent she could hear the sound of her own footsteps. After which came the darkening and darkened stairs, and the door of her room that was never quite shut and never quite open, within which stood table, chair, and bed, waiting, like friends. She moved suddenly, and the bed creaked.

Negations sometimes claw at her, especially when she remembers the tiniest things. The bell that remains unanswered, and the office press that will not quite close, an unstamped and forgotten letter, and got up and slowly fingered through the few books on her shelf, one of which she picked up and held to her, then opened, and read upon its flyleaf, 'Gan Tad-Cu, Geraint Vaughan', and turned its pages one after another, idly, thoughtfully, finally lowering her eyes to read the quotation that followed.

And with a long, slow smile, she closed the book. She thought of a man that had stared at her, long and penetratingly from a chapel pulpit, a stare so vivid that she had immediately closed her eyes against it, and walked out, and none since had ever seen her enter the Penuel chapel. He came even clearer to her now as she stood in front of her

37

mirror and looked in. A man dressed entirely in black whom she now knew as one Mervyn Thomas, a minister in the town. Once he had followed behind her all the way to the office, and another time she found him standing opposite the Decent Hotel when she returned home. And he had smiled, and she had not. She had heard Jones talk of him with Mrs Gandell, and of his sister, 'Perhaps,' she thought, 'Mr Thomas depends on smiles.'

She went to the door and opened it wide, and stood listening. Mrs Gandell was actually singing to herself in the kitchen, but Jones himself seemed silent. She supposed that at any time now she would hear that call to lunch. Immediately she put on coat and hat and gloves, picked up her handbag and went downstairs and straight out of the hotel, only to bump into Jones at the first corner she turned. He stopped dead and stared at her.

'Why? Miss Vaughan! Well indeed. I thought you were resting. I thought you were having lunch with us.'

She noted the parcel tightly hugged under his arm. 'I am going for a walk,' she said, and passed him by, and Jones hurried back to the hotel.

Mrs Gandell was waiting for him, and seized the parcel and hurried off with it to the kitchen, to return a few moments later with a cigarette in her mouth, and a glass of gin in each hand.

'Sit down,' and Jones sat down.

'I thought you were never coming.'

'But I did come, didn't I, Mrs Gandell. I did my duty.'

She flung him a cigarette which he lit, and they drank each other's health.

'Everything's ready, Jones.'

'Good. Good.'

'She won't be long now. Perhaps you'd better give her another shout.'

'Who?'

'Who on earth d'you think?'

'I hardly know, such abruptness, Mrs Gandell.'

'Go and *call* her.'

'Call *who*?'

Mrs Gandell, glass at her lips, screeched, 'Miss Vaughan. Who else?'

'She's gone out.'

'Gone *out*?'

'Passed her in the street, nose in the air as usual.'

'You amaze me.'

'She amazed *me*.'

'But she said ....'

'Said not a word to me, Mrs Gandell. I asked her how she was, and she said she was quite all right now.'

'But lunch was *arranged* ....'

'The logic of the situation is as follows,' said Jones. '*We* will eat it all up ....'

'I can't understand her,' Mrs Gandell said.

'Does it *matter*?'

'So extraordinary, Jones.'

'Nothing is extra*ord*inary, Mrs Gandell. Iesu mawr! I keep *telling* you that. Do brush the sawdust from your ears,' and Jones laughed, since for him, Gandell in a predicament was always a sight to see. He got up abruptly and went off to the kitchen.

'And bring the bottle,' she called after him.

'Will do.'

They ate in silence for a whole five minutes.

'She may indeed have come here because nobody else would have her, Jones.'

Jones was far too involved in his lunch, he didn't bother with a reply.

'I was speaking to you.'

'I heard,' snappily.

'Well?'

'Well what, Mrs Gandell?' and slowly his head came up.

'Oh ... nothing ... it doesn't matter?'

'Then stop worrying. Be like me, say nothing and accept everything.'

39

'I am not like you, Jones.'

'Pity,' Jones said, tittering, then bent to his meal.

A momentary silence, and then Mrs Gandell remarked casually that the town was talking about them.

'About who?'

'Us.'

'There you go again, worrying. The town has a very large mouth, Mrs Gandell.'

'Give me that bottle,' and he gave it.

She helped herself to another glass of the fortifying gin.

'You simply love that stuff, don't you, Mrs Gandell?'

An observation she refused to confirm, and pushing away her plate she ordered Jones to remove everything to the kitchen. He carried out the loaded tray, and she sat back in her chair and lit another cigarette.

'Dis*gust*ing,' she thought. 'What on earth could Miss Vaughan have been thinking of? Ordering lunch, and then walking out on it.' She could hear Jones threshing his way through the dishes and pans. And then the smile came, as it always did after the third glass.

'Jones!'

'Coming.'

'Sit down, Jones.'

He sat down. She seemed to be looking, not at him, but at his person.

'What are you staring at, Mrs Gandell?'

'Your jacket,' she said. 'You'd better get another one at Davies's when you go in this week.'

'Very well. But I still like it,' he said.

'I don't.'

He walked across the dining-room, surveyed himself in the mirror.

'Thanks, Mrs Gandell,' he said, and returned to the table.

'For God's sake don't keep on *thanking* me,' she said.

'I do what I want to do,' he said.

He picked up the glass, and then the bottle. He held it

high to the light.

'What a noble flash lies therein, Mrs Gandell,' and he helped himself to another drink.

The most awkward situations, the most ordinary situations hold their desperation, and they both knew this, on a flat morning. She held up her own glass, gave him a sudden smile, and said, 'Your health, Jones.'

'That's the third time, Mrs Gandell,' he said, refusing to smile.

He leaned across to her, she felt the quick squeeze on her arm, as Jones said, in a wheedling tone, 'I am sure that you are looking forward to crossing the frontier, Mrs Gandell,' and went on squeezing.

She kissed him with a wet mouth, took his hands. 'I always look forward to you doing your duty, Jones.'

'Lovely.'

'I'm sorry about last night,' Jones said. 'I do have my moods.'

'Don't we all,' she replied.

He noticed that her speech was beginning to thicken, he sat back in his chair. The gin began to dribble on her chin, the hand with the glass was shaky, and he quietly removed it. 'Yes, you like crossing the frontier, Mrs Gandell,' he said, accepting without thanks, her expanding smile. 'I'll set you on fire.'

'Will you, Jones?' and the smile stayed.

'Soon,' Jones said, 'soon,' leaned across again, patted her hand.

'You are very good to me, Jones,' Mrs Gandell said, and for the hundreth time, 'I wouldn't know what to do without you.'

Jones was so glad that he gave her another drink, and then helped himself. And for the fourth time they toasted each other's health. He had begun to stutter, but she was quite blind to that.

'Do - - d'you know what they call me in this town, Mrs Gandell?'

'Wha - - - what do they call you - - - - Jones?'

'I - - I - - I'll *tell* you,' said Jones, and he loved the great, coarse laugh that followed.

'Th - - th - - they call me an emanation, Mrs - - *Gand* - - ell.' He gave a loud titter, adding, 'Think of that. An emanation. Think of it, an e - - - man - - a - - - tion.'

'Wh, wh - - what is that?' she asked, and would have dropped her glass had he not deftly caught it.

'What it *is*,' he said, and grinned at her.

He sat well back in the chair, he noted the high flush that had come to the Gandell cheeks. He lit a cigarette, spread legs, picked up the bottle and replaced the top. 'Enough is enough.'

Mrs Gandell made to get up, but sat heavily down again. Jones watched, Jones smiled, the language was old, and he knew all the words.

'Soon, Mrs Gandell,' he said, 'soon.'

She made to rise again, grabbed the table.

'Did I tell you that the man with the chariot in his head has written Vaughan another letter, Mrs Gandell?'

She shook her head, leaned heavily on the table.

He stood up, leaned over her. 'I'll re - - - re - - read it to you after we've crossed the frontier, Mrs Gandell.'

'A l - - le - letter,' she said.

'A letter,' Jones said.

'You - - you - - you've been in - - her room, Jones.'

'I always empty her wastepaper basket,' he said, and he leaned very close to her and hissed, 'And you *know* that.'

Suddenly her head was heavy on his shoulder, and he was stroking what was vast in her.

'Ah,' he said, 'ah!' And he stroked, and went on stroking. 'She never reads letters. I *told* you,' and felt her breath in his face as she stuttered her reply.

'Oh - - - yes - - yes, of course - I remember now. I *see*, Jones.'

'Glad you do,' he said. 'I have to tell you things so *often*, Mrs Gandell,' and against her ear, added, 'Sometimes I

42

think you've a brain with the fragility of a wren's leg.'

She seemed unaware that he was speaking, and she had closed her eyes, and only knew that he was actually *there* by reason of a geographical exploration across her flesh.

'Shall we?'

'Yes,' she spluttered, and was heavier still, on the slight, iron, yet nervous Jones shoulder, her faithful servant.

'*Come* along,' he said, and raised her up, and took her total weight, and at a list of twenty degrees staggered with her across the room, and at the foot of the stairs came to an abrupt halt. She had an overwhelming desire to sit down, and sat down, and Jones knelt in front of her.

'You could cross *now,*' he said, '*here,* or we can go upstairs.'

She flung her arms round him. 'Upstairs, Jones.'

'Soon, I'll send colour flying into your Yorkshire mug, Mrs Gandell,' and as he leaned heavily against her glanced up the long flight of stairs, that in this moment seemed to stare back at him with a hint of menace.

'Soon,' he said, 'soon.'

'Ah,' she sighed, and gave him another wet kiss.

And always remembering his manners, his *place,* Jones said, 'Thank you,' and after some effort, managed to get her on her feet, and then began the slow ascent of the stairs towards that *other* room that could never be Miss Vaughan's.

'Jones,' she said.

'*Mrs* Gandell,' he replied.

And inch by inch, and stair by stair, until they finally reached the top. She swayed, and he caught her, turned her the right way round, slowly pushed. He kissed the Gandell ear as they reached the door.

'Soon,' he said, 'very soon. And then the explosion, Mrs Gandell, and much better than a mere collision. Yes, indeed.' She promptly sat down again, and refused to budge.

Jones knelt, her face between his hands.

'It could never be said that yours was a handsome face,

43

Mrs Gandell, but it's kind, I mean *kind*, and that's the square root of something better, yes indeed,' and he patted her on both cheeks, and stroked her hair, as he whispered, 'We're on the threshold of our moment. I'll do my duty, and you'll do yours. Simpler than plain fractions. Ah! But I have been obliging to you. Just think of the occasions when I've made you feel twenty-five, and lifted you far away from that struggling widow, and the outlandish place from which she came.' He put his arms round her. 'And you can really tingle when you want to, Mrs Gandell. So here we are together, so high up, and remote, and safe, and silent, and cuddly, and warm. I can see the signal in your eyes, the words, the mes*sages*, dear Mrs Gandell, light of my ordinary life.'

He got his hand to the doorknob, he turned it, and they both fell in. He pulled her to the bed, he heaved her into it, and then sat down.

'Jones,' she said, and Jones came, and lay across her, and said, 'We are about to cross. D'you know, the first time I ever saw you, I wondered where your leg ended. I did indeed. Close your eyes now, my dear.'

The fierceness of her embrace quite staggered him.

'At last,' she said, 'at *last,* Jones.'

'Ssh,' he said, 'ssh!'

'Jones,' and it was hot in his ear.

'What, Mrs Gandell, *what*?'

'I wouldn't care if I never went down those stairs again,' she said.

'Wouldn't you really? *Um*! Ah . . . .'

'Jones?' she said.

'What?'

'Jones,' she spluttered, 'For once I am *not* Mrs Gandell,' and she pressed closer and closer, and suddenly the fiercest whisper in his ear. 'Sometimes, Jones, I positively hated you addressing me like that.' Jones could not, and did not hear, lost and abandoned as he was, yet safe and warm at the harbour of her feeling.

44

'Um . . . .'

'Ah . . . .'

'Grist mawr! This *must* be what they call the end,' muttered Jones, the words as soft as water in her ears.

'Ssh,' she said, 'ssh!'

And then the silence, the light beginning to go, the dusk coming down. The clock in the corner struck the hour, but they did not hear it. Beyond the window clouds were suddenly rampant as a fresh wind blew in from the sea. The silence arched. She stirred slightly, but Jones lay motionless, his moment crowned. And then the faintest whisper from her lips, the fairy breath.

'Jones!'

Hot and abrupt in his face, against his still closed eyes, but he made no answer. Her fingers wandered in and out of his hair, ran down his back and up again, encircled his neck, but not a move nor a sound made. Jones was deeply sleeping, beyond the frontier of the world. And a warmth, a tiredness was suddenly pressing upon her own eyelids, and easily, casually, like a child, she, too, was sleeping. The clock struck four, and darkness was full and home. They seemed scarcely breathing.

They did not hear the sound of a key turning in the lock, nor the steps in the hall, nor the creak on the stairs, as Miss Vaughan climbed up to her room, opened the door, and switched on her light. She sat down on her bed, and sighed. The short winter afternoon had died behind her, in various places, and she had had lunch. When she left the hotel she had walked direct to the little railway station, and had sat for nearly an hour on one of the two iron benches that the station boasted, before she was noticed by the fussy station master, who came up and spoke to her. A winter afternoon seemed scarcely the time to sit watching the trains move in and out. It had seemed to him such an odd thing to do. Surely she could not be waiting, perhaps for the last train in the world.

'Excuse me, madam,' he said, and sharp enough to make the lady jump. 'Excuse me, but are you waiting for a train?'

'I am not.'

'For somebody coming to the station?'

'I am not,' Miss Vaughan said. 'Thank you,' and got up and walked away leaving the bewildered station master staring after her. She walked the length of the main street, staring into window after window, and one or two chilly faces looked out curiously at this fugitive of the afternoon. She had then walked right out of the town in the direction of the beach. Perhaps Miss Vaughan was in love with winter.

3

And, quite unknown to her, the man in black, suit, raincoat, and Homburg, had faithfully and silently followed behind her. A dumb devotion had experienced a most uncharitable afternoon, for not once did Miss Vaughan turn her head, and, even had she done so, and caught his smile, she would not have answered it. Miss Vaughan was like that, private.

'I smile at her, but she never smiles back.'

And he watched her walk out of the town, towards a distant shore. 'She looks so unhappy, *lonely,*' he thought.

He liked Miss Vaughan, he liked her greatly, he was sure that he could make her happy. He had never quite forgotten that first glance of hers as she stood at the back of Penuel, and even in recollection her too sudden departure was still felt as a shock. He had stood watching her until she finally vanished in the mist, and he had turned round and walked slowly back to his home, the derelict return to his study, and thoughts of many notes in his head. What a strange afternoon it had been, that lone traveller, and he behind her, whilst the rest of the town hugged its fires, and listened to the wind in the chimney. A silent woman. A lonely woman. *Surely*? And living in that awful hotel. What on earth had made her go to such a place? Where had she come from? The thoughts crowded in on him, as heavy and slow as tumbrils, and he stirred and stirred at the tea his sister had brought to his study.

'I wish . . . I wish and I wish,' and then he drank his tea. He knew the Decent Hotel, he knew that woman, knew that attic room where Miss Vaughan lived, knew that 'Welsh fragment' Jones. Ah!

A tap on his door.

'More tea, Mervyn?'

'No thank you, Margiad.'

He heard her sigh, heard her walk away. He closed his eyes, rested his head in his hands. He thought about Miss Vaughan.

'What great big eyes daylight has, Miss Vaughan.'

He swung his hat in his hand, he listened, he breathed heavily, and waited for the answer. But the silence seemed that of mountains, powerful, stupid. He waited, behind a blue curtain, at the top of the stairs. A bedroom door was closed.

'Who is that?'

It came to his ear like an echo.

'Only me.'

'*Again*?'

'Again.'

'What do you want?'

'I could make you happy, Miss Vaughan. You know that.'

'I *am* happy.'

And the words dragged, 'Is *that* all?' the voice sepulchral.

There was no answer. He rested on one leg, and then the other.

'Did you have a nice dream last night, Miss Vaughan?'

'I like dreaming.'

The promptness of reply astonished him.

'I - - er - - -' he stuttered.

'Are you still *there*?'

'Once upon a time, Miss Vaughan, there was a hard-bitten and winter man that walked out of a turnip-cold field, and took a great hurricane lamp to the barn, and lighted it, and hung it up. After which he walked home to his supper, and thence to bed. His bones ached after the long day, and he slept deeply. And he was *real*. You are not quite real, Miss Vaughan, yet I know I could make you happy.'

And again he listened, waited. A too sudden titter quite un-nerved him.

48

'You are full of grace at eight o'clock in the morning, Mr Thomas.'

'Is that *all*?'

And another titter. 'Was there something else, Minister?'

'I am myself, Miss Vaughan, yes indeed. And I am the only one that notices you as you walk down the street. Who else does? The world? Who *cares*?'

He expected a further titter, but the silence was total.

Words stabbed into the darkness. 'Have you finished?'

'Today will be like yesterday, Miss Vaughan, and the day before that, and tomorrow will be no different. Not for you, a *great* pity. I often think of you.'

'Thank you.'

'And you are welcome, Miss Vaughan.' He paused, and continued nervously, 'Miss . . . .'

'You will never find me,' she said.

'I shall not keep you, for I know the world is waiting. Yes indeed.'

'Are you gone?'

'I am not gone.'

'Then *go*.'

'I know the girls at your office, Miss Vaughan, I've seen them there.'

'*Go*.'

She did not expect the hushed whisper, but she heard it.

'Some of the girls are young, Miss Vaughan, and some are threatening to be older, and there is one that must often think of her own pre - - - *car* - - - ious age.'

'I am *not* listening.'

'You *are* listening. You are always listening, for you have the ears of a hare, even in your *dreams,* you are listening.'

He came erect, he stiffened. The silence seemed endless.

'Surely you are not *still* there?'

'If only I could open the little door in your head, Miss Vaughan. Ah! I'd know then what it is that keeps your head so high, so *far* away. Your bed is *cold,* Miss Vaughan,' he paused, '*P*o - - - lar.'

When the next titter followed he let his hat fall from his hand.

'I really thought you'd gone,' and she spoke so quietly that he had to strain for a sense of the words.

He heard movements in the room, and he still waited, listened.

'Once, a bishop said to me, Thomas, I see the church triumphant in your face, but in your own, Miss Vaughan, I sea an ocean of loss.'

The reply was prompt, wholly unexpected.

'Is there no *end*?'

'There is no end.'

'Mervyn!'

The rude shout, the abrupt hammering on his study door struck him like a blow from a fist, and he sat up, rubbing his eyes, pawing at the collection of notes in front of him.

'*Me*rvyn!'

And angrily he shouted back, 'Who *is* that?'

The door burst open, and there she was, his sister, Margiad.

'I've been knocking this past minute, what on earth is the matter with you, Mervyn?'

She stood on the threshold, stared at him. His hand passed slowly across his brow, the words fell like stones.

'I must have been dreaming,' he said.

'D'you know how long you've been sat there?' she asked.

'I - - - *don't* - - - *know*.'

'Is something wrong, Mervyn?'

'Nothing is wrong.'

The tiredness in his voice brought her closer.

'What is happening to you, Mervyn? Tell me. Something is wrong.'

And the voice, now hollow, said, 'Nothing is wrong.'

'I . . . .'

'Nothing is *wrong*, Margiad. Dreaming, that's all. I *told* you.'

'There's some things you never tell me, and I am your sister.'

'I know you're my sister, and I know you're good to me,' he replied aggressively.

'Then don't be *long*,' she snapped, turned on her heel and slammed the door behind her.

Thomas sighed, picked up the notes from the desk, pored over them.

'Must've nodded off, yes, that's it, dreaming, strange, stra - - -' And the man with 'the chariot in his head' began rubbing his eyes again, staring about him, then his hands fell heavily to his lap, and he kneaded them and thought, 'Dreaming. That's all.'

He had been so bent, and close, and concentrated on his task. Mervyn Thomas was always most careful about what he wrote, and, too, he liked his own style. Then the door had burst open so suddenly. 'Margiad,' he exclaimed, but when he looked up the door was closed. Her voice was distant, yet penetrating. 'I suppose you *are* coming in for your supper?'

'I'm coming.'

'D'you want the cake I made yesterday?'

He got up and stood fingering the doorknob. 'I will have it.'

He staggered rather than walked into the sitting-room, and saw his sister stood at the small table by the fire that she had just laid.

'How queer you look, Mervyn,' she said.

'Queer?'

'I said it,' she snapped, and sat down, and beckoned him to do the same.

She served him. 'What is the matter?'

'I told you, nothing.'

She leaned across the table, stared. 'Are you sure about that? And it is now ready for Sunday?'

His voice tired again, the words dragged. '*Yes*. Said it,' and, after a pause, casually, 'I just dropped off whilst I was doing my notes about Cain's terrible deception of a loved brother. And *that,*' he concluded, stabbing his plate, 'is all.'

'I see. You will have the cake, Mervyn?'

He sighed. '*Yes.*'

'I'd an idea you'd fallen asleep in there.'

'I dozed *off.*'

They continued their supper.

'With your collar off, Mervyn, you look no different to me than other men.'

And he said nothing.

'You did not even say the grace,' she said.

And he said nothing.

He avoided her penetrating stares, he hurried on with his meal, and then got up, and sat in the big chair by the fire, collected a pipe from the rack, and filled and lighted it. He then lay back, relaxed, and closed his eyes.

'Strange indeed, Mervyn,' she exploded.

He looked across at her. 'I'm sorry, Margiad. I just forgot.'

'You should *not* forget that, and it seems to me you are forgetting a number of things lately. You seem not to be yourself.'

'I am quite - - - all - - - *right.*'

'Others may not think so,' and she got up and began clearing the table.

'What others?'

She stood over him, the filled tray in her hands. 'The world,' she said, and went out and left him, and now he hunched a little, drew nearer the fire. 'Ah,' he sighed, 'ah!'

She came in and sat opposite him, picked up her knitting, and settled herself comfortably. He puffed contentedly at his pipe.

'You were late again last night, Mervyn,' she said, but did not look up from her knitting.

'I was rather late.'

'And the night before that,' she said, 'and this afternoon.

I am not blind. I do not like it,' and she let the knitting fall to her lap.

'A lovely fire, Margiad,' he said, and offered her a smile. 'You are very good to me.'

'Your tongue hasn't always got such silver in it,' she snapped, and picked up her knitting again, and attacked it with some vigour. She was always ready with the questions, readier still with the answers.

'And you?' he asked.

'What about me?'

'Nothing.'

'There's a meeting at Penuel tomorrow afternoon,' Margiad said.

'I see.'

'Glad you do.'

'Good.'

'And you?'

Speaking very slowly, he said, 'I shall be going out also.'

In an instant she was standing over him. 'Again?' she asked. And he dropped the cold stone. 'Again.'

'I'm surprised.'

There was a long pause, and then he said quietly, 'Margiad, I will tell you something. I am sometimes sad.'

'Then it will do you good.'

'Sometimes, I say to myself, "Mervyn Thomas, your life is like fragments".'

'Then lock them together and you'll be your own self again.'

'Ah!'

'Sense will come, Mervyn, though I hope it will not come too late.'

He leaned forward, put a hand on her knee. 'Please,' he said, '*please.*'

'Mari Richards saw you walking in the town yesterday.'

'Those sharp eyes miss nothing, Margiad.'

'You were even seen talking to that shrimp, Jones, from the Decent Hotel.'

53

'What on earth are you talking about?'

'What am I talking about? You know right well, Mervyn. Drunk again, they say, and you know what *he* is when he's in his cups. That man would turn himself into a thousand and one nights and talk your head off. He'd put knots in one's very soul. Imagine talking to such a person. *You,* of all people, Mervyn.'

'There are some things that you do not understand, Margiad.'

'Tut, tut! What nonsense,' she replied, and, looking thoroughly disgusted, concluded, 'and at *your* age.'

'At *my* age,' he said gravely, and relighted his pipe.

'You're a fool.'

'Perhaps I am, and perhaps I am not, Margiad, but you are good to me, and I'm grateful.'

She made to rise, but didn't, then flung the words at him. 'Yes, *you,* and God on your tongue Sundays.'

On which he got up and went slowly across to the window, opened it, and put his head out. And the silence infuriated her.

'It will do you no good,' but he made no reply.

She too, got up. 'I am *talking* to you, Mervyn Thomas, are you listening?'

It seemed an age before the reply came. 'I am listening,' he said, and pulled his head in, closed the window, and returned to his chair.

'Sad it is to me, Mervyn, people coming to me, talking. A disgusting one, that Jones. Sat on his bottom in The Lion most evenings, where does he get the money? From her, of course, and you know right well whom I have in mind. Sleeps in her bed for his wages, a cringing, crawling shadow of a man. Yes, I *am* worried in my mind about you, Mervyn.'

'He is after all, only a creature, Margiad, like you and I.'

'Never stops laughing behind your back.'

'What I think, I *know*, what I say, I *mean*,' he said.

'It's my life that is fragments, not yours.'

'Have *you* finished?'

'I can't believe it.'

'I shall be going out at eight o'clock.'

'I'm glad they're laughing at you.'

'And you are still my sister, and I say again, you are good to me.'

But again she was standing over him, and suddenly he thought, 'How angry she is,' and drew away from her.

'You really are going out then?'

'I am going out, Margiad, and that is *enough*.'

He watched her put away the work-basket. How she fussed about things. But then, she always did.

'I shan't be long.'

And at the top of her voice she shouted, 'I am not your warder.'

'Indeed you are not. You are my sister, and that is all.'

'I will not wait up.'

'Understood.'

'You will find me where I am, Mervyn, and that is respectable.'

'I shall not disturb you.'

'You are a *fool*.'

'Do I say thank you to that?'

'I wish I could *laugh*.'

He rushed at her, screamed in her face, 'Then laugh.'

Margiad sat down, bowed her head, twisting her fingers in her lap. She made to look up at this brother, but did not, and then said quietly. 'If this goes on much longer, Mervyn, your chapel will empty.'

The outright laugh quite shocked her.

He was bent over her, suddenly grinning in her face.

'Talking like a prophet now, are you,' he said.

The moment he caught her glance she closed her eyes, and sat further back, and deeper down in her chair.

'Have you thought of Mr Price?'

'I have thought of a good many things,' Mervyn replied.

'I always took you to be a sensible man,' she said.

'I have learned to be humble.'

'You are still a fool.'

'I'm not ashamed of being a fool.'

'I'm only surprised that you cannot hear the laughing in your ears.'

He returned to his chair. 'Is that all?' he asked. 'There is nobody laughing, Margiad.'

'You *mean* that.'

'I mean that.'

'You'll be a disgrace to your collar.'

With a tired voice, he said, quietly, 'I cannot hear you, Margiad.'

'You're ill, and you don't know it. I'll have Dr Hughes here to see you. I mean that.'

He got up, went across to her, was close again, and this time the flat of his hands pressing on her shoulders.

'*Will* you - - - leave me - - - *alone*?'

She removed his hands, stood up, faced him, her mouth opened and closed, but she said nothing, but stared at him with a look of utter bewilderment.

'Do sit down, Margiad,' he said, and pressed her back to the chair.

'I don't know you, you're a changed man, something's happening and I don't understand it. Your years are toppling you, Mervyn.'

'Once, I was afraid of myself, think of that. Me, a man.' He stood back, 'And now I'm not. I'm going out.'

'They'll laugh louder than ever.'

'Let them laugh.'

'That one at the Decent Hotel read a letter you wrote, and they laughed their heads off about it.'

'Who told you that?'

'Mari Richards . . . .'

'Her again,' he exploded.

'Tegid Lewis, The Lion, told her. She heard it from that God's fright, Jones.'

'He's a liar.'

'Tell him that.'

'I'll break his back with a word.'

'Break it.'

He flung his hands into the air. 'What is the matter with everybody?'

'Perhaps Mrs Gandell laughed loudest, the English sometimes do.'

'She is an English bitch,' he said.

She clapped hands to her head, covered her face. 'Mervyn! *Mervyn!*' She rose, then pushed him away, and made for the door, at which she turned, and said, 'I think you're going mad, Mervyn Thomas. I can't believe it. Once the words were like lambs at your lips, but not now, no, not now. The change in you these past months, it makes me sad, I mean *sad*. It's like a stain on this house.'

He rose and walked the room, up and down, and she still stood there, angry, frustrated, ashamed. She made to speak and could not. Half way across the room he stopped.

'How *bitter* you are,' he said.

'Not bitter. *Sad*,' and her voice faded out, 'that's all.'

'There's somebody knocking.'

'There's nobody knocking.'

'There *is*,' and quite involuntarily, screeched it at him.

'I'm going now.'

'*Go.*'

She moved aside and he reached the door, and then she rushed after him, caught his hands, and looked hard and long at this changed brother. Her voice suddenly lost its outright harshness, the anger. 'I was thinking last night of my father's house, of your own mother, Mervyn, shining with goodness she was,' and she gave a heavy sigh. 'It's a long road indeed to travel and find only stupidity at the end of it. You, a *grown* man.'

Very quietly, he said slowly, 'Perhaps the desert will grow between us.'

'One day you'll return to this house and find that I am not here.'

'You will always be here, sister, I know that, as I know that you are a good person,' and he went out into the hall.

She immediately followed, and again caught his hand as he opened the front door. 'Wait,' she cried, 'wait.'

He turned and said roughly, 'Well.'

'Listen,' she said. 'I remember one in my own father's time, that was just like you, his head turned by a bitch, and had this terrible storm in him when the knife was showing in his years. Yes, and you knew him, too. That man's pride fell away from him with a terrible thud, Mervyn, a *terrible* thud. Lifted beyond your height, Mervyn, that's what it is. Now . . . you tell *me* something.'

He only closed his eyes and stood silent, his fingers trembling on the doorknob.

'Well?'

And he was silent.

'*Yes*, silent, that's you, you can't *see*, can't *hear*, you're stuffed with a vanity that can only be laughed at. Yes indeed, you remember that man, and I remember him, too, as I recall the echoes in his chapel that grew louder and louder, and nothing left for him except the miserable sheepdog that whined at his heels. Her voice faded, became hollow. 'There was no one else, there was nothing, I mean nothing, *emp*ty, cold, *lost*, so foolish he was, so *driven*. One day you'll be nothing, and you'll remember the day that I said it to you, Mervyn.'

He stepped down into the street. It had begun to rain.

'I will not be long,' he said, and he walked off into the darkness, and she stood there, peering after him, and heard his heavy, halting steps in the deserted street. She slammed the door and went straight up to her bedroom. She sat in the darkness, and thought about her brother. Perhaps she, too, should get up and go out, into the air that was cool, into the silence. She thought of going down and continuing her knitting, and already she could hear the rhythmic click of the needles. Her thoughts rocked. Perhaps it would help calm her. But she sat on in the darkness, undetermined, bewildered, sad.

'Perhaps I'd better go down,' she thought.

But everything seemed bewildering, and everything was strange. She shut her eyes, sat stiffly, twiddling her fingers.

'I don't *know*,' she cried, into the empty room. And she didn't. 'How things change, life, people, words, and now . . . this. Like a wound in the house. How can he be so silly, at his age.'

She went down, made herself comfortable by the fire, resumed her knitting. The needles clicked, the fire spat occasionally, and outside the rain poured down in the darkened town. And as she knitted she thought of their lives, the order of their days, the peace, the acceptance of what was right. She thought of the Penuel, *his* life.

'I wonder where he is, now, at this very moment?' And suddenly she was thinking of rushing out, looking for him, bringing him home. 'No, no. I couldn't do that. Not nice.'

She thought of the odd-job man at the Decent Hotel. Jones, Islwyn Jones, and she remembered her first glimpse of him as he came out of the back entrance of The Lion. Decent Hotel indeed. It would not last long.

'Ah well,' and she got up and went into the kitchen and put milk into a pan, and sat and watched it heat. When it was boiled she returned to the sitting-room. From time to time she glanced up at the clock, thinking of Mervyn, worrying about him. Where does he *go*, what does he *do*?

She threw down her knitting, went to the window, opened it, and looked out.

'How late it is.'

And the hammering thoughts came back, the distant words, and the near ones, and always the rumours.

'Very soon I shan't be able to lift up my own head.'

She stiffened the moment she heard a key in the door.

'At last. He's back,' and she rushed back to her chair, forgetting to close the window.

He entered the room so quietly that before she realised it he was standing in front of the fire.

'You're tired, Margiad,' he said gently, and looked down at her with not a little concern. 'Bed, sister, bed.'

She got up. 'There you are then, Mervyn.'

'Here I am.'

'I thought I was alone in this house.'

He bent to her height. 'And you are *not* alone, Margiad,' he said.

He went into the hall, hung up his raincoat.

'Any supper?'

'There is milk in a pan,' she said.

And later heard him pottering about in the kitchen.

'Thank you,' he said, and then a call, 'is this all. Just milk?'

'Just milk.'

'Oh! I see.'

But she made no reply to that.

'I'm sorry you're angry with me, Margiad,' he called, then came in with milk, and some bread, and sat by the fire, and began his last meal of the day.

She was still standing there, leaning against the mantelpiece, staring down into the fire.

'Go to bed,' he said.

'You're living in the clouds, Mervyn Thomas,' she said, and bent down and vigorously poked the fire.

'Is there no way in?' he asked.

'No way,' she said.

'Ah!' And he sipped slowly at the milk, and even smiled at her.

'Be upright, and you'll find the way,' she said.

He put down the mug, sat back, folded his arms, studied her. He felt sorry for her. 'Do go to bed now, Margiad.'

'I will go to bed,' but she did not move.

After a short silence, she said, 'The wind's been roaring in this chimney half the night, but then you would never have heard it, no.'

'It was wild outside,' he said.

'Once, I nearly went out myself,' Margiad said.

'In the pouring rain?'

And she flung the reply at him. 'It's the same rain that hammered your shoulders,' she said.

'Well? And what of it. And what *now* Margiad?'

'I've watched, I've waited, I've prayed, Mervyn, yes, and hoped that a word would melt on your tongue. You're ill, brother, and I'm much worried by it. I *wish* you'd see Dr Hughes. He is clever, and will help you.'

'Leave me alone, for God's sake.'

'For whose sake? You'll be left alone, have no fear of that. Come now, Mervyn, it's you that should get off to bed, not me. Wet through you are. What a mad dream you're living, you *silly* man. Be sensible, Mervyn, come now, get off to bed. And you look very tired.'

'I am not *tired*.'

His laugh frightened her. 'I don't want to be sensible. Just leave me alone. You go to bed, I'm all *right*, Margiad.'

'It's that bitch,' she shouted in his face.

He got up, went close, '*Will* you leave me *alone*?'

'The look in your face, you're threatening me,' she said.

'I'm threatening nobody, I just want to be left alone,' he said.

'I saw that one once, yes, close as close. Oh God! When I sit and think of the peaceful days at Hengoed, and now this one comes here, turning you into a real fool. No peace at all now, ashamed, that's what I am, all these weeks, the days long, and the nights longer,' and she sat and buried her face in her hands.

For a moment he thought she was going to cry.

'I've asked you to leave me alone,' he said.

'I'll never do that, never. It's nearly midnight. Did you know that? If I went out this moment I would see only a single light shining in all this street. This one, this house,' and she threw her arms round him, crying, 'Mervyn, *Mervyn*.'

He broke free and rushed to the door, but she was behind him, and now barred his path. 'I wish to God I could cry about it.'

'Then cry, *cry*,' he shouted, and suddenly she appeared to go limp, clutching at the door, and he heard the break in her voice.

'I'm sorry, but I cannot help it, Margiad,' he said.

She was livid with anger, and for a moment he thought she might even spit at him. He went into the hall, and she followed after.

'I really begin to think my sister is hating me,' he said.

'She's a *whore*.'

She saw his shoulders slump. 'And that is the living truth of it, brother.'

He did not move, seemed hardly to realise that she was still there and then he glimpsed her hand searching for his own. 'I wish,' she began, 'I wish . . .' but the remaining words froze upon her tongue.

He made as if to go, but did not move; he wanted to look so closely into her eyes, to feel her breath upon his cheek.

'D'you remember, Mervyn, how once, in the cool of an evening, we would go out and walk to the top of the hill and look down the valley. But not now, no, not now.'

She drew away from him, as if in an instant she realised that she was too close to something beyond her comprehension, and was in this very moment afraid to touch. He watched her move slowly back into the sitting-room, and, on reaching the chair, collapse into it. He thought he heard a sob, yet remained motionless, staring down at the carpeted hall.

'Good night, Margiad,' he said, 'and God bless you. Sleep well.'

His hand found the knob, and the turn of it sounded thunderous in the silent house. Through spread fingers his sister stuttered, 'You - - - you - - -'

He turned and looked back at her, but said nothing.

'Not even a light in your room these nights, Mervyn. Sitting in the dark you are, so still and silent. Perhaps you're afraid to look into your mirror, of what you will see, locking yourself up in a mad dream.'

He moved, stopped in the threshold.

'Very soon things will be too late. You'll wake up when the laughter crashes in your ears.'

She heard the door close.

'In God's good time he'll be left alone,' she thought.

She started to dampen the fire, locked the doors, shut the window, and turned out the light. Climbing the stairs seemed endless. She passed his room. It was in darkness. And no door had ever seemed to slam shut with such resolution, as though it were now closed forever. She slipped quietly into her bedroom, undressed in the dark. She knew she would not sleep, and remembered how late one night she had seen the light still burning in his room, and going there, had found him slumped in his chair, still dressed. Wasn't he going to bed?

But he had remained dumb, motionless, indifferent. She thought of it now as she tossed and turned in her bed. Was he, even now, sitting in that chair, and all the emptiness about him? She got out of bed, crept along the landing, quietly opened his door, and looked in. She leaned forward, listened.

'Poor man. Silly man,' she said to herself.

The curtains were fully drawn, the darkness black, and the heightened silence seemed to give to the room another dimension. She crept back to her bed, and lay there, wondering, wishing, hoping. If that woman had *never* come. If that hotel had never opened. If Jones had never been born. If only they were back at Hengoed, happy in those other days, and Mervyn safe in his purpose, safe with his duty.

'I could go and see Dr Hughes in the morning.'

She got up, and quietly opened her window. It had ceased raining.

'I could talk to that woman. Yes, that would indeed be best.' And suddenly Mari Richards was talking in her ear.

'Yes indeed. I *know*. Queer it is, Margiad, queer, your brother like that. I saw that woman from nowhere, in the Penuel that night, close to her I was. Duw! She looked like one that has been lost for a hundred years, and your brother staring, staring. And no one saw her come. Works for that Mr Blair, say she has no friends, wants none, and holds her head very high up whenever she passes a girl from his office, and often goes walking along the shore, all by herself, and that Islwyn Jones told Tegid Hughes that she stays in her room and keeps her door shut tight, and Tegid said to him perhaps Minister Thomas wants to marry her for her money, very keen he is, always following her around, once he tried to speak to her. Mr Blair likes her because she is very quiet and works well. Mrs Blair once asked her to tea, but Miss Vaughan said she had a prior engagement, whatever that would be, I don't know. Strange, isn't it, Margiad.'

And the words rocked like many tiny boats inside her head, and she turned and turned in her bed, and again she thought of Dr Hughes, reaching out to him with imaginary hands, wishing him to come, to talk to her brother. So sad and silly, all of it, no peace now, and people talking about the good man that might be walking too near a rocky road, and leaving God Almighty behind him, that was even worse.

When she closed her eyes she saw immediately the vivid green of a place called Hengoed, her brother walking a lane, and the 'good mornings' crowding in on him as he went on to his chapel. Not so much rain at Hengoed, and the sun more kind. She lay still in her bed, memory a balm, a child voice sharp in her ears, a smiling brother beside her at the festival.

'Ah!' and she gave a great sigh, and thought again of the next room, and the utter silence and stillness.

'In the morning, first thing, yes.'

64

The very words filled her with resolve, and yet with a certain dread, remembering a chapel that was far off, and in the evening time a tall man bending low to a dog. 'I will save you,' and the shout through a smashed window at the other end of it. 'Save *yourself*.'

She opened wide her eyes, looked up at the ceiling. 'Poor man.' No, it must not be like that, finger close to a madness, and she could see him with clear open eyes, coiled in a chair, one that would not sleep.

'Poor Mervyn.'

She struck a match to look at the clock. Half past two.

And not a sound from that room. Such a change in him, so sudden, so violent. She closed her eyes, muttering to herself.

'Tomorrow I will go and talk to Mr Hughes. That is *it*,' and, knowing it was final, suddenly fell asleep.

In the next room, still sat, Mervyn Thomas pondered on his life.

4

Mrs Gandell was happy, she was fulfilled, but the star that had risen on that terribly ordinary afternoon fell the very moment she opened her eyes.

'Jones!'

There was no answer.

'*Jones!*'

Jones woke suddenly and cried, 'Yes, what now?'

'Are you awake?'

And he said flatly, 'I'm awake, Mrs Gandell,' and he sat up, opened his eyes, and felt the very darkness in which he drowned.

'Good God!' he cried, 'I'm on the floor, Mrs Gandell.'

After the crossing of frontiers, after the explosion, Mrs Gandell had conveniently kicked him off the bed, where he had lain flat on his back, legs widespread, gently snoring.

'Put that bloody light on, Mrs Gandell.'

She switched it on just as Jones got to his feet, and beheld her resting on one elbow, smiling across at him. He came towards her.

'What happened?'

'You must have fallen off the bed, Jones. And now you had better get down, hadn't you. There's the evening meal.'

'How practical you can be when you want to,' he said.

'Very,' she said, and added, 'and tomorrow there is much to do. The windows, the rooms, the dining-room.'

She lay flat on her back again. 'And don't be too long, Jones.'

Jones cursed the darkness, and then the too sudden light, and finally the clock.

'Look at the time,' he said.

'You look at it,' she said, 'and do hurry.'

'Am hurrying,' he replied, and completed dressing. 'What is it?'

'You know what it is, Jones. *Stew.*'

'Oh yes, of course.'

'Do wake *up*, Jones.'

He leaned over her and said menacingly, 'And you? What about you? I'm not the only one with duties.'

'I shall be down shortly,' Mrs Gandell replied, and turned her face to the wall. She heard the door bang, his flight downstairs and later much noise from the kitchen.

'I would really like to fall asleep again,' she told herself, taking with her the afternoon dream, shutting off tomorrow. But she got up and slowly began to dress. She sat herself at the dressing-table, inspected herself in the mirror.

'I'll have to replace Dooley soon.'

She would send Jones down to the Labour, and see what they had on hand. But no more Irish. She had had enough. Jones was in the dining-room when she came down.

'The draughts in this room are getting worse, Jones.'

'I noticed that.'

She followed him into the kitchen, and they leaned to one another as she inspected the evening meal.

Suddenly she clutched his arm. 'Jones!'

'What, Mrs Gandell,' noting the tone in which she spoke. 'What?'

'Miss Vaughan.'

'What about her?'

'I haven't heard a sound.'

'Neither have I,' Jones said, and casually went on staring.

Mrs Gandell clapped a hand to her mouth, stared stupidly at Jones.

'What's the matter?'

'A horrible thought just came into my head,' she said.

'*What* horrible thought?'

'Suppose she hasn't come back?'

'Hasn't – come – back, Mrs Gandell? What the hell are you talking about?'

She gripped his arms. 'Suppose she just went off, like *that*,' she said, flicking finger and thumb, 'suppose she *never* came back?'

'Oh God!' he said.

He saw that she was worried, he knew that she was angry. But surely the worst could not *come* to the worst. No indeed. He brushed his lips against her cheek, and said quietly, 'I'll go up and see. And remember how quiet she is, Mrs Gandell, hardly makes a sound, just one of the big mouses here.'

She gave him a push. 'Do go up, Jones,' and when he had gone she rushed into the dining-room, sat down at their table, and thought of the worst. 'If Miss Vaughan went . . .,' but she could take the awful thought no further, and sat drumming the table, waiting, listening.

'I just forgot all about her. Yes, and then her not coming in to lunch,' and she rushed to the bottom of the stairs, waiting, listening. She dreaded to call out to him.

And as she stood there the afternoon happiness was miles away, and facts as big as fists were coming her way.

'Jones!'

There was no answer.

'Jones?'

He came tiptoeing to the top of the stairs, and asked breathlessly, 'What, Mrs Gandell?'

She sent a hushed whisper upwards. 'Is she back?'

'I'm just going to knock,' he said.

'Then hurry up. Perhaps she's asleep.'

'Perhaps,' he said, and disappeared down the landing.

Then she went back to the kitchen, and did not notice the letter lying behind the front door. She concentrated on the steaming pans. She taunted herself, challenged. 'No, oh no. She couldn't do such a thing. To go off like that. No, Miss Vaughan was far too nice a person, and more important still, at this very moment, her only asset.

Jones, meanwhile, was gently tapping on the Vaughan door. He listened. Not a sound. He tapped again. And then, like Mrs Gandell, he, too, feared the worst. 'She's gone. Cleared out. The mean little *bitch*.'

'Miss Vaughan!'

He leaned his head against her door.

'Miss *Vaughan*!'

'Who is that?'

Jones gave a great sigh. 'It's me, Miss.'

'And who are you?'

It made Jones jump. 'Me, Jones, Islwyn Jones that was, is, and forever shall be. Are you there, Miss Vaughan?'

And the voice as soft as velvet. 'Of *course* I'm here.'

'I'm glad,' he said.

'Are you?'

He thought he heard the tiniest laugh from inside the room.

'Are you all right, Miss?'

'I am quite all right.'

'I'm, I mean we're glad. We were worrying about you.'

'Was Mrs Gandell worrying?'

'*Course* she was, Miss.'

'People that worry are silly, Jones,' Miss Vaughan said.

Jones fingered the doorknob. 'You really are all right, Miss Vaughan,' and hearing no reply began tapping on the door again.

'What is it?' and he caught the irritation behind it.

'It's supper time, Miss Vaughan. That's what. Mrs Gandell is waiting downstairs. Terribly worried about you she was.'

'Mrs Gandell is silly, Jones.'

'Will you come down now then, Miss Vaughan,' and without realising it Jones had fully turned the knob and the door slowly opened.

'You seem to be worrying, too, Jones,' Miss Vaughan said.

After which there was a silence. Curiosity made him put his head slowly into the room. Miss Vaughan was lying on her bed, a book in her hand.

'Well indeed,' he thought, 'it's only me, Miss Vaughan,' he said.

'You told me that.'

She was hidden behind her book, and now slowly turned a page. He wondered how she could read in such a poor light.

'Your supper'll get cold, Miss,' Jones said.

And he stared at the motionless woman on the bed, who calmly turned yet another page. His head went further in.

'Not a very good light, is it? Shall I ask Mrs Gandell to put in a brighter one? You must notice it when you're reading, Miss.'

'I never notice.'

'Oh!'

Miss Vaughan turned another page, and forgot that Jones was there. He was now fully visible on the threshold, his eyes everywhere, taking in bed and table, mirror and books, table and tiny clock.

'You are coming, Miss?' he said urgently.

'I am *coming*, Jones. Isn't that enough?'

'There is a letter for you on the floor,' he said.

'Leave it.'

'Yes, Miss. Then I'll tell Mrs Gandell you'll be down soon,' and suddenly Miss Vaughan was looking at him, over the book, over her spectacles, and then she calmly turned another page. Jones shot downstairs and positively flung himself into a chair.

'Gone?'

'No. She's there, Mrs Gandell. Everything's all right. Still with us.'

'Thought you'd never come down, Jones, that the worst had really happened. Just the sort of person that would.'

'She's coming down shortly. Knocked three times and she didn't answer. I thought she'd scooted, then I knocked again, and it was all right. She must have been in all the afternoon. And d'you know what?'

'What?'

'I think she has a mood on, kind of queer, she was fully stretched out on the bed, reading a book. Never even looked at me when I put my head in, she was hidden behind it, and even while I was there actually read and turned two whole pages. Asked me some odd questions did Miss Vaughan, so being decent, I gave her the oddest answers. But it's all right, she's coming to supper. Said she had her lunch at the Blue Bird Cafe today.'

'I hope she enjoyed it. How lucky she is to have such a decent employer.'

'Told her we'd kept her lunch for her, waited an hour, she said nothing, never even apologised, Mrs Gandell, just went on lying there, reading, still as still . . . .'

'Stupid woman,' Mrs Gandell said.

'It's only a mood,' Jones said, 'we all have moods, don't we?'

But she did not answer him, and looking at her he realised how greatly relieved she was.

'If she had beat it, never come back, it might have been worse.'

'I'll call her.'

And she called from the bottom of the stairs, in her best bosun's voice. 'Miss *Vaughan*! Are you coming, or *aren't* you. Supper is getting cold.'

Miss Vaughan's voice seemed to come from a great distance.

'*Com* - - - - ing.'

'Bring it in, Jones.'

'Yes, Mrs Gandell.'

He served them both.

'Here she is now,' he said. 'And by the way, Mrs Gandell, I found this letter under the door.'

'Ah!' and she cried out, 'It's Mr Prothero, Jones. Think of that. Coming here next week,' and she read on, '*and* he's bringing another guest with him.'

'How splendid,' cried Jones. 'How splendid,' and they

rose and embraced each other, just as Miss Vaughan appeared at the top of the stairs.

'Serve her.'

'Yes, Mrs Gandell.'

'Good evening, Miss Vaughan.'

'Evening, Mrs Gandell.'

'Sorry you were not in to lunch today. Hope you're better now.'

Jones hovered, served, bent low, smiled, and Miss Vaughan sat right back in her chair.

'I am quite all right now, Mrs Gandell. Thank you. I had some lunch at the Blue Bird Cafe, and after that I went for a long walk by the sea.'

'How nice,' Mrs Gandell said, and concentrated on her supper, Jones likewise.

'You like the sea, Miss Vaughan?'

'Love the sea.'

'I hope you'll enjoy your supper, Miss Vaughan.'

Miss Vaughan looked across the room, smiled, and nodded gravely, then continued her meal.

'Mr Prothero is coming next week,' Mrs Gandell said.

'Indeed!'

'And bringing a friend, too.'

'How nice for you,' Miss Vaughan replied.

Mrs Gandell leaned across to Jones, and whispered, 'I'm still annoyed with her, Jones.'

'Of course, quite right. Just wasting the food, that's all. The day isn't a bad penny after all, Mrs Gandell. Two guests coming next week. Things are looking up.'

He waited for a response, but none came. 'But they really *are*,' he said. 'You're not eating, Mrs Gandell.'

'I think I'll go up, Jones,' she said, 'I've rather a headache. I shall leave my faithful servant to do what is necessary, and don't forget to lock up.'

'Of course.'

When she rose, he rose, when she walked across the room, he followed.

She stopped at the Vaughan table, looked severely at her guest, took a vacant chair, and sat down. 'You don't mind?' she asked.

Miss Vaughan smiled, and said, 'Certainly not, Mrs Gandell.'

'Your supper all right?'

'Yes, thank you.'

'Good. Then please, another time, let me know in advance if you are not coming in to a meal.'

'I'm sorry,' Miss Vaughan said, and Mrs Gandell got up, and again Jones was behind her. He watched her climb and vanish.

He went back to his table, and finished his supper. Out of the corner of his eye he watched Miss Vaughan. She had taken off her spectacles and was cleaning them.

'Coffee, Jones,' she called.

'Certainly.'

He brought the coffee, and served her.

'That's the very first time I've seen you with your glasses really off, Miss Vaughan,' he said, but she made no reply.

'Miss Vaughan?'

'Yes?'

'May I sit down here?'

'If you wish.'

'Thank you.'

'Well?' she said.

'Mrs Gandell has gone to bed, Miss. Headache. *Actually*, she was a bit upset at your saying one thing and meaning another . . . .'

'Indeed!'

'Well, she had got ready your lunch, Miss, and then you never turned up.'

'I see, Jones.'

'Yes. Things are a bit difficult for her at present, Miss Vaughan. Mrs Gandell was saying to me the other day that you don't go out very much, that you seem to have such few friends, nobody ever calls here to see you, and

73

you get hardly a letter in the post.'

'Well?'

The abruptness of the question quite stumped him. It rang out like an ultimatum, and Jones stuttered, 'Nothing, really. Mrs Gandell just hopes that you are satisfied with everything. We are not the Ritz or the Hilton,' he said, and smiled at her.

She looked at him, and said slowly, 'I am not complaining, Jones.'

'No, Miss.' He paused for a moment, and then added, 'Once, Mrs Gandell was looking at you, sitting alone at the table, and she thought you looked lonely, Miss Vaughan. Mrs Gandell always thinks of her guests.'

'Thank you, Jones.'

'Welcome. You don't go to Penuel now, do you?'

'Not now,' she said. 'Do you?'

'Sometimes.'

'I heard you both laughing in your room this afternoon,' she said.

'*Did* you?'

'*Yes.*'

'Those that never laugh are strange, Miss Vaughan. But I'm sure you know that. As a matter of fact we heard you laughing yourself the night before last. Some people laugh in their dreams,' and he sat back in the chair.

'More coffee, please,' she said, and she watched him go to the sideboard.

'Thank you.'

'I was sorry to hear about your father,' he said. 'Mrs Gandell was telling me about it. I think Mr Thomas knew him once.'

'Mr Thomas?'

'That's right, Miss,' and suddenly, 'have you a mother, Miss Vaughan?'

'Have you?' she asked.

'She's in another kingdom, Miss,' Jones said.

'Oh!'

'Yes, Mr Thomas was telling his sister the other day that he liked you. Have you met his sister?'

'No.'

'I passed their house early this morning, Miss, Ty Newdd it is where they live, and I looked through their window. I like looking through windows. It was only eight o'clock, but there she was sitting by the fire, knitting his socks, and her lips were moving all the time, praying for him, I expect. He's very close indeed to God Almighty, Miss. I expect he was in his study, *very* fond of his study he is. *She* looked sad.'

'Sad?'

'Worried about her brother, Miss.'

'Some things are sad, Jones.'

'Funny, I mean that you should have heard us laughing this afternoon. Very close I was then to Mrs Gandell, *very* close. I once walked behind Mr Thomas, all the way to the post office, and he didn't see me at all. He's a very busy man, like St Peter he is, always fishing with his nets . . . .'

'Do you dream, Jones?'

'Me! No, never. Sometimes, when I'm too close to Mrs Gandell, I wish I could. D'you know what, Miss? I read through a whole book every week. She likes that. Imagine it, a whole book.'

'I won't imagine it,' she said.

'No, Miss.' He pulled out a cigarette. 'Do you mind, Miss Vaughan?'

She shook her head. She shook it again when suddenly he offered her one. He leaned so far across the table, and so abruptly, that she drew back, picked up her handbag, and seemed bent on a sudden departure.

'You weren't laughing, Miss Vaughan,' Jones said. 'You were *scream*ing.'

'*Was* I?'

'Yes. We heard you.'

She leaned to him and said in a hushed voice. 'I hope Mrs Gandell is not worrying about me, Jones. Sometimes

75

I catch her looking at me in rather a strange way.'

'Mrs Gandell worries about all her guests, Miss Vaughan.'

'Mr Thomas's sister came to see her yesterday. Very worried she was.'

He paused, watched, waited for reactions.

'She's afraid of losing her brother.'

'Indeed!'

'She told Mrs Gandell that her brother is in love with you.'

And Miss Vaughan gave out a loud, and prolonged titter.

'*Really?*'

'Really. He thinks you are lonely, Miss, and very unhappy.'

'I *am* happy,' she said.

'Good. Then Mrs Gandell and I are both glad to know that. We do not like our guests to be unhappy. Did she tell you you could have the larger room now?'

'I have my room. I like my room. I've told her that, Jones.'

'Do you like Mr Thomas?'

'I laugh at Mr Thomas,' she said.

'*Do* you?'

'I laughed when he came to my room,' she said.

'*Came* to your room? What happened?'

'I laughed.'

'Actually went up to your room? How did he get in?'

There was the tiniest laugh. 'I never asked him,' she said.

'I can't believe it,' said Jones, 'I can't.'

'It didn't matter.'

He watched her fidgeting with her handbag, studied her hair.

'Very plain really,' he thought, 'but nicer with those specs off. And the way she looks at you, straight at you, through you, and that pale calm face. H'm! Must be forty, perhaps forty-five, yes.' And the question hammered at him. How did Thomas get *in*?

She put her bag on the table, looked at Jones. 'There,' she said.

When he leaned across the table, she leaned back, and his hands gripped the table.

'Talking of screaming, Miss, if anybody starts screaming *now* its bound to be her upstairs, yes indeed. D'you know what?'

Miss Vaughan didn't, made to get up, then sat down again.

'Can't bear me out of her sight for a second, fact. There's skin-close for you, Miss. Once, I said to her, "Mrs Gandell, sometimes you're too real for me." I once hit her right across the jaw. Know why? Started calling me Fido, just as if I was her little dog.'

'I saw the Colonel yesterday,' Miss Vaughan said, her voice hushed, confiding.

'If hardly *anything's* real to a person, Miss Vaughan, would you say they were lucky?'

'It's a long long way down the shore,' she said. 'I love the shore, Jones. He has a big house down there.'

'How very nice,' and he lit a cigarette. 'Very nice indeed.'

'He always locks his father in the house before he comes down to meet me,' she said.

'Which Colonel, Miss?'

It was the very first time that he had heard Miss Vaughan giggle.

'You'd like to know,' she said.

'Only knew one Colonel myself, and he used to live up at a place called Y Briach, but he's dead now, so wouldn't be yours, would he?'

'Sometimes we have lunch together,' she said.

'I *am* glad,' said Jones. 'Thought you'd no friends at all, Miss. Very important to have some friends.'

She very abruptly took out a puff, and began slowly

powdering her nose.

'D'you like to know things in advance, Jones?'

'I don't like to know anything in advance, Miss Vaughan.'

'You look positively bewildered, Jones,' Miss Vaughan said, smiling.

'Do I?'

'*Yes.*'

Her bag clicked shut, she got up, and Jones rose with her.

'Glad you enjoyed your supper,' he said.

'I expect Mrs Gandell is really glad to have me, Jones,' she said.

'*Very.*'

They crossed the room together. 'Back to your room then, Miss?'

'That is where I live,' she said, and slowly climbed the stairs.

Jones remained rooted, stuttered, 'Yes, of course, well, good night, Miss. Sleep well.' He began to clear the tables.

'How very odd,' he said to himself, 'very odd indeed.'

And backwards and forwards he went, and in the kitchen began to wash up. 'How the hell did that man get in?' And then, 'But *did* he get in? Did she imagine the whole thing,' and he washed and wiped, after which he went back to the dining-room, relaid the two tables. 'I wonder if Mrs Gandell knows anything about this?'

He checked on the windows, and the doors, picked up the transistor, turned out the light, and went upstairs.

He was surprised to find Mrs Gandell sat in a chair by the window that was partly open. She heard him come in, close the door, felt him behind her. He leaned over, stroked her shoulders.

'How's the headache, Mrs Gandell?' in the gentlest of voices.

'Not too bad,' she said. 'Has Vaughan had her supper?'

'She has.'

'I've been think about her, Jones.'

'So've I.'

He collected a chair and sat beside her, he took her hand in his.

'I'm still annoyed with her.'

'Understood.'

She turned suddenly, 'Oh Jones! Am I glad Mr Prothero's coming!'

'And his friend, too,' Jones said, and gave her a warm smile. 'That's splendid news, Mrs Gandell, really splendid. Perhaps the ice cracked when we weren't noticing. That Miss Vaughan was telling me she never notices anything. Think of that. Ah well, its actually the beginning. That'll be three guests next week. Marvellous.'

'I very nearly told her to pack her things and go, Jones.'

'*Why?*'

She felt his hands stroking her knees.

'There's something about her that I dislike,' Mrs Gandell said, 'and yet I just don't know what it is. Something.'

'She is a bit strange, I know, but if she coughs up the cash, Mrs Gandell, why on earth should we worry.'

'I should say very odd, Jones,' she said.

'But she's not much trouble to us, well is she, and she pays her board in advance, and no trouble at all really. She goes off in the morning and comes home in the evening, she has her supper, then goes up to her room. Finis. *Simple.* Don't you agree? Any other place would welcome her with open arms.'

Suddenly she put an arm round his neck, pulled him down.

'You wouldn't leave me, Jones?'

'What a silly bloody thing to say to me, Mrs Gandell, we'll never leave each other, and that's the way it goes.'

'Thank you, Jones.'

He gave her a quick kiss. 'That's all right,' he said.

'I'd like a drink. And get me an aspirin.'

'I'd get you anything, Mrs Gandell,' and he went to

the corner cupboard and took out the bottle, and two glasses.

'I'm afraid the aspirins are in my office.'

'Nuff said,' replied Jones and immediately went out.

She got up, pushed back the chair, and stood looking out of the window.

She looked up at the stars, she saw a glittering sea, she heard the wind. She thought it would rain again soon. 'I'm anchored here,' she thought, 'nailed.' She went to the mirror, sat down, began fidgeting with her hair. She switched on the small light above it, and looked at herself in the glass. She looked fifty-five, *knew* she was fifty-five, her hair was greying, her skin had become sallow, her eyes dull, and she leaned in and examined herself more closely. Yorkshire seemed deserts away. She was split in two. 'I had hoped for so much.'

When Jones returned she was still sitting there, then suddenly he was right behind her, and the too sudden sight of him made her switch off the light. She got up and went to the fire.

'Everything locked up, Jones?'

'Everything, all correct and shipshape, Mrs Gandell. Here, take these, and I suggest you take the gin hot. I've put some sugar in it,' and he bent over her, and smiled, but she did not return it.

'You are sad,' he said, 'knew you were, knew it all this long day.'

She sipped the gin, offered him a faint smile. 'Sit down, Jones,' and for one awful moment dreaded him saying, thank you.

'Not still worrying about *her*, surely?'

'I wasn't even thinking of Miss Vaughan,' she said.

'Then what?'

'My life,' Mrs Gandell said.

'You know I'd be very sorry indeed if you were unhappy, Mrs Gandell,' Jones said, and she was touched by that.

'I'm glad you're here, Jones. Nobody else would have stayed in this miserable little place, its not a hotel really, just a small boarding-house. When I came here I had hoped for the best.'

'Never stop hoping,' he said, 'never. I don't.'

'Please,' she said, holding out the glass, and he gave her another drink.

He was stroking her knee again, smiling, leaning close. 'Don't be sad, Mrs Gandell. After all we did get some good news, didn't we?'

She nodded her head, made as if to smile, but didn't, and he noticed her hand was shaking.

'You're not ill, Mrs Gandell?'

'I'm not ill.'

'Thank God for that.'

'I can't even explain, not even to you, Jones, how I feel this very moment. I feel empty.'

He turned from her, stared into the fire. She *had* changed, all in a flash. But why? 'And when my boat docked in her harbour this afternoon, why, she was as happy as the day is long.'

'It's been a lousy winter, Mrs Gandell, a long worrying time for you, and who knows it better than I do. But it's not the end, never is, really.'

She reached out and took his hand. 'You have your kind moments, Jones.'

She wanted to shriek when he said quietly, 'Thank you for that, Mrs Gandell.'

'I don't think I'll ever forget this winter, Jones,' she said.

But Jones said nothing, but picked up the poker and rudely disturbed the fire, sending up the flames. This return to what he called 'her winter theory' positively irritated him, and he continued poking at the fire, until she finally pulled the poker from his hand.

'There'll be no fire left if you go on,' she said.

'Sorry,' and he felt her hand on his shoulder.

'I once felt empty, Mrs Gandell, *really* empty, just like

you do now, awful feeling, like everything seems to stop suddenly, you're kind of locked in, can't even take one single step outside yourself. Ah,' he said, 'ah,' stroking her cheek, willing her to smile, and he was right back in the afternoon, hearing her laugh, and then the words in her ear, velvet soft.

'But you won't give up, will you?'

She shook her head.

'*Sure?*'

She smiled an answer, and it cheered him up.

'What you feel, I feel, what you know, I know,' Jones said, and then followed up with an extra warmth. 'That Tegid Hughes at The Lion always asks after you when I call there. He's very obliging, I must say. Only place that is in this potty little town. You must never feel empty, Mrs Gandell, ever feel *outside*, ignored, left. Please don't. I hate you being sad,' he paused for a moment, and then said, 'Mind if I have another,' and she didn't, and he got himself another drink. 'How about you?' he asked.

'No more,' Mrs Gandell said.

Her sudden change of mood still intrigued him, and he wondered about it, and, deep down he was afraid of it, remembering the early morning, the broad hints. Surely she wouldn't break her promise, sell up, *go*? He wanted to get close again, to probe, to find out.

'That bloody morning mood, that worrying about the bank again,' and he wanted to shout, 'God Almighty, the winter won't last forever.' Jones was like that, and always aware that the compass points of his world were the four walls of the Decent Hotel. Their near regular guest, Mr Prothero, had once christened it that, and Jones had signed and sealed it. But Mrs Gandell preferred its original name, Cartref.

'How quiet it is,' he said, breaking the silence, but Mrs Gandell appeared not to hear, and sat very still, and stared into the fire. And Jones thought of the order of his days, and was content. Unlike Mrs Gandell he accepted it all.

Monotony was merciful to Jones.

'Shall we go to bed, Mrs Gandell?'

But there was no answer.

'I could read to you if you like,' he said.

The Gandellian thoughts were miles and miles away. He leaned over her. 'Come along, Mrs Gandell. Let's go to bed, get close, get warm.'

He waited for a move, a sign, but she seemed gone off on a journey, and he would not restrain her.

He got up. 'Going to bed now,' he said, and began to undress.

He sat on the bed, removed his shoes, all the time watching her. When at last she rose and came towards him, he gave a sudden sigh that did not escape her. The country of the flesh beckoned.

'Good,' Jones said, 'Good.'

5

Back at Ty Newdd Mervyn Thomas had brooded half the night, tossed and turned in his bed, and thought about Miss Vaughan. If only she would smile, if only she would speak to him. He lay in the darkness, oblivious of the time, of the noisy activity in the kitchen below. 'Am I bad? Am I too good? *Why* can't I make her happy? What is wrong with me?' But the questions remained unanswered, and when his sister shouted up the stairs, 'Breakfast,' he sat up and switched on the light. 'She *is* lonely, I know it, I feel it in me. I . . . .'

'You coming,' and then the rapping on his door.

'All right, all right, Margiad, I am not deaf,' and he got up and dressed. 'Strange,' he said, looking at the clock. 'So early for Margiad.' When he went downstairs his breakfast was already laid out for him. And she was there, waiting, sphinx-like, and seeming to look in every direction except his. And, unusual for her, she did not say good morning, and served him in silence. He sat down.

'Anything wrong, sister?'

She did not answer.

'I hope you slept well, Margiad,' he said.

'Well enough.'

'Good. I'm glad of that.'

'And you?'

'I had a very good night.'

'You must be off to Llys this morning, Mervyn. Twice now you've forgotten to see old Miss Pugh, you must do your duty. And she expects you to do it.'

'I will do that, Margiad.'

'I'm glad.'

'I'm sorry that you were so upset last night, Margiad,' he said.

She did not answer, but finished her tea, and got up, and went straight up to her room. He continued his breakfast, and had already forgotten a lady by the name of Pugh. When she came down again he was surprised to see her dressed and ready to go out.

'You're going out very early, sister,' he said.

'I shan't be long.'

He half rose as if to see her to the door, but instantly sat down again.

'And you will *not* forget Miss Pugh,' she said, turning on her heel at the door.

'I will not forget.'

She flung her reply across the room. 'You forget too many things.'

'I wish to heaven, Margiad, that you would not upset yourself in this silly way. And how much better if you *tried* to understand.'

'The town understands.'

'Paper come?'

'I didn't look,' she said.

'Any post?'

'None,' and she went out, slamming the door behind her.

'*Very* unusual for her,' and he suddenly remembered their conversation of the previous evening. 'Good heavens, no. She can't have gone off to see that Dr Hughes? I won't see him, I won't. Stupid woman.'

But Margiad Thomas was already bent in that direction, a crusading light in her eye, resolute of purpose, determined. And at this very moment was sitting in the waiting-room, among the coughs and colds, the pains and aches, and just long enough there to find her neighbour's severely asthmatic breathing something of a trial. It was the very first time she had even been in a doctor's waiting-room, for Margiad Thomas would have beamed had you told her that she was as full of good health as she was of sense.

'Miss Thomas?'

She looked up, and there was the smiling receptionist. She got up and followed her across the corridor. 'This way,' and paused at the door and knocked. 'A Miss Thomas, doctor.'

'Show her in.'

Another smile, and Miss Thomas was suddenly facing the doctor, already studying her over his pincenez. 'Do sit down, Miss Thomas.'

'Thank you,' and he was quick to note her stiffness of manner.

'What can I do for you?'

'It's about my brother, Doctor.'

'I - - - see,' dragging the reply. 'Have we met before?'

'Some years ago, really,' Margiad said, and would have liked to have been proud, and added, 'of course my brother Mervyn, is also very healthy.'

'You're not ill?'

'Oh no, Doctor.'

'Good. Now about your brother, Miss Thomas?' and he sat forward and looked closely at her.

A matron with a prim look, well dressed, wholly at ease save for the continually twitching fingers in her lap.

'Tell me about him? Is it urgent?'

Miss Thomas leaned to him. 'My brother has become a changed man, Doctor. In these last weeks his whole character has changed. He is really not himself, and I'm worried about him. There's something wrong, he's not well.'

'Continue.'

She leaned even closer, dropped her voice, and continued: 'Ever since a certain woman came to this town, Doctor, to work for that Mr Blair, the solicitor, he has been a changed man. He forgets things, neglects the parish, and is hardly ever in the house.' The loud chatter from the waiting-room penetrated Dr Hughes's ears.

'Could you be more explicit, Miss Thomas, there are others waiting?'

It was a whisper that followed. 'He doesn't sleep well at

86

all, some nights I look into his room, and there he is, sat in his chair facing the window, still dressed, and often in the darkness . . . .'

'How old is your brother?'

'Fifty this year.'

He respected the anxiety all too visible in her face. 'Thomas, Thomas,' he thought, 'surely not on my list.'

'If I could have some pills for him, doctor . . . .'

'Is he on my list, Miss Thomas?'

'Yes, Doctor.'

He got up and began running through the files in the cabinet.

'Some rheumatic trouble, five years ago, correct?'

'That's it.'

'I'll give you something that will help him to sleep at night,' he said, and thought to himself: 'Following a woman, what woman?' He wrote out a prescription and handed it to her. 'There!'

'Oh! Thank you, Doctor. I'm sorry to have bothered you, never wished to, really . . . .'

He waved it all away, and asked, 'Following what woman, Miss Thomas?'

'A Miss Vaughan, she's staying at that little hotel, Cartref, at present . . . .'

Laughing, he said rather boisterously, 'Never heard of her,' and he rose when she rose and showed her slowly to the door, suddenly put a hand on her arm. 'Miss Thomas!'

'Yes, Doctor?'

'You're not imagining all this, are you?'

'Oh no,' she replied indignantly, 'No, Doctor. I wish you'd see my brother, I really do.'

'There are such things as rumours,' he said, smiling. 'Very well, I'll arrange to have a talk with him. By the way, isn't he the Minister at Penuel. I have heard about some very good sermons there.'

Margiad positively beamed. 'That's it. Knew you'd remember, Doctor.'

'Don't worry' he said, opening the door, 'it never helped anyone.'

'No, Doctor, thank you.'

The smiling receptionist led her to the front door. 'Good morning.'

The receptionist put her head in just as the doctor called, 'Next, please,' and as she went out, asked, 'Do you know Miss Thomas?'

'Never heard of her.'

'Or a Miss Vaughan staying at Cartref in Prince's Road?'

'Never heard of her,' the receptionist said, and went out again, and he heard her call out, 'Miss *Davies*?'

'Miss Thomas should take some pills, too,' he thought, as he rose to receive his next patient.

Miss Thomas was still standing outside the door, looking anxiously up and down, as though not quite certain as to the direction she should take. She felt disappointed, she had expected more, and got less, she did not like Dr Hughes's manner, he had seemed to dismiss the whole thing with a mere toss of the head. He had seemed indifferent, not caring.

'He is a very busy man, I know.'

'Ah well,' and she felt a sense of relief at having done her duty by her brother, and she looked forward to his calling. Mervyn would be angry, but then he had been angry, and moody, and totally incomprehensible these past weeks. Something had to be done. People passed by on their way to the town, there was the occasional 'Good morning' in her ear, and 'Out early this morning.' The town had sharp eyes, and missed nothing.

'Morning,' Margiad would reply, staring at the pavement.

She felt imprisoned in this street, and then a hand touched her arm, and she turned violently to find her friend, Mari Richards, smiling in her face.

'Nicer morning than yesterday, Margiad, awful, wasn't it?'

And Margiad stuttered, 'Yes, it was, wasn't it?' and

walked quickly away, to the astonishment of her friend, who, going her way, stoked the fire of her own imagination.

'Very odd indeed, at *that* time of the morning,' she thought, staring after the rapidly distancing form of Miss Thomas.

'Of course, it's that brother of hers, that's it,' visualising the morning when a man wearing a white coat would call and take Mervyn away. 'Well, well!'

Miss Thomas was glad to slip into the first cafe she came to, to sit down, to order herself a cup of coffee, and even more glad to find the place empty. Even the girl coming forward to serve her was a relief. She looked up at her. A total stranger.

'Yes, Madam?'

'Coffee, please.'

'Certainly.'

And she accepted the coffee, and the mercenary smile that accompanied it. 'Anything else, Madam?'

'No, thank you.'

And watched the girl suddenly vanish behind the blue curtains at the end of the room. She sat over her cup, slowly stirring, wondering, asking herself questions, answering them. Had she done the right thing? And what on earth did that doctor think he was doing, asking if she had imagined it all. Of *course* she'd done the right thing, and she sipped quietly, and looked out of the window at the people passing by.

She put down the cup, thinking, 'Perhaps I could go and see this Vaughan woman myself,' but instantly dismissed it from her mind, her pride stiffening. No. But there was this Mr Blair, the solicitor, for whom she worked. Perhaps she could talk to him. When she turned away from the window she saw the girl's face between a chink in the curtains. It made her call at once.

'Another cup, please.'

'Thank you.'

If *only* she had never arrived in the town. Yes, she

would see Mr Blair. But how to avoid that woman? In a sudden desperation she even thought of seeing Mrs Gandell herself, thought even of Jones. 'I *wish* I knew what best to do?' Saw her brother mad, heard the laughing town, and her hand trembled as she put the cup to her lips.

When she looked up the girl had gone, she was alone again. And even as she sat there, the cafe seemed to have grown suddenly larger, and the blue curtains more distant, the silent, invisible assistant even more silent. She longed for the feel of a hand, longed for the words that might come, reassuring as open arms, and she stared around the empty room, and listened to the tick of a little blue clock on the shelf above her head. Eleven o'clock. 'I've been out two hours, and nothing has happened, *nothing*,' and suddenly she was lost and drowning in her own dilemma. She did not hear the ring of the bell, nor see the door opening, nor the tall man that entered and sat down at a nearby table. And there was the assistant hovering over him in an instant, with a fresh smile.

'Morning, Mr Blair.'

'Good morning, Nancy. Usual, please.'

'Certainly, Mr Blair.'

Margiad Thomas jerked upright, stared at the man. 'Blair. Blair. Of course, yes, the solicitor, *him*.' The small miracle over the horizon in a moment, and again her hand shook, and she spilt some coffee, and she continued to stare at this tall, well-dressed man.

'He could tell me everything,' she thought.

'Good morning,' she blurted out, and the head turned, there was a momentary pause, then the man smiled, and said casually, 'Ah, good morning, Miss Thomas. And how are you today?'

Margiad sat bolt upright. 'I am very well, Mr Blair, thank you.'

'Good,' he said, and settled himself to his Horlicks and his biscuits.

Should she ask him? Shouldn't she? She watched the girl

disappear behind the curtains.

'D'you think the weather will improve, Miss Thomas?'

'I hope so. Terrible its been lately.'

And cup at his lips, Mr Blair, replied, 'Yes, first time I've seen you at the Blue Bird,' he said.

She dropped her voice, stuttered, 'Yes, I had to see Dr Hughes today.'

'You're not ill, I hope.'

The words gave her strength, a sudden way in, and she smiled, but said nothing, too surprised as she was, then got up and walked slowly to him. She bent across his table, and in a whisper, asked, 'Could I speak to you for a moment, Mr Blair?'

He looked up. 'Of course,' and he motioned her to the opposite chair.

'Thank you.'

She sat with her back to the blue curtains, again dropped her voice, and said, 'If I could talk to you in confidence, Mr Blair, I would be most grateful.'

He sat back, studied her. 'Is something wrong?'

And again the conspiratorial whisper. 'I'm worried in my mind, Mr Blair.'

'How is your brother?'

'Not well at all,' she said, and the reply leapt out.

'Oh! Dear, dear! I'm sorry to hear that, Miss Thomas.'

'Ever since a certain woman came to work in your office, my brother has become a changed man.'

'Indeed!'

'You have heard the rumours no doubt, Mr Blair. I will spare you my own feelings. You've met Mervyn, you *know* him, but you would not do so now,' and her sudden sigh seemed to fill the room.

'Sorry to hear that,' he said, and then felt a sudden tug at his coat sleeve.

'My brother is following that woman about, Mr Blair, people are watching, talking about it, and the rumours . . . .'

'*Rumours*?'

She was astonished at the sharpness in his voice, 'What rumours? What is it you are talking about, Miss Thomas? I hear no rumours. What is all this?'

Her voice seemed to come from a distance as she said very quietly, 'He follows her about everywhere,' and paused, as though awaiting a fresh wave of her own confidence. 'He's a changed man, and he's hardly ever at home now.'

With some irritation Mr Blair pushed away his plate. 'Who *is* this person, Miss Thomas?'

'A Miss Vaughan, Rhiannon Vaughan, I understand.'

'What about her?'

And tentatively Miss Thomas whispered close to his ear, 'I wondered if you could tell me anything about her. If only you knew how sad this is for me, Mr Blair.'

He sat back in his chair, and she was startled by his sudden change of expression, and lowered her head.

'A Miss Vaughan came to see me from a small village in Dynbych,' he said, 'I had advertised in a paper there. She is a typist in my office. She works well, and is very reliable, and that is all that I require from any employee of mine, Miss Thomas.'

'Is she . . . .'

'I never discuss the private life of my employees with anybody.'

'They say she has no friends at all, and hides herself in her room all the time, and sometimes is seen walking by herself along the shore.'

'Miss Vaughan's life is Miss Vaughan's business,' Mr Blair said. 'I cannot discuss her with you. What your brother does is your brother's business, Miss Thomas, and what Miss Vaughan does is hers. I hope I have made myself clear?' He paused for a moment, then leaned very close, and said abruptly, 'And that is an end of the matter.'

And now she clutched at both coat sleeves, and said in a fierce whisper, 'Mr Blair, my brother is a Minister of *God*.' The silence was sudden, Mr Blair seemed relaxed, nibbled at his biscuits, sipped his Horlicks. He disliked this quite unexpected confrontation.

'I'm ashamed,' she said, and he felt her tone fierce, and close.

'There is no morality today, Miss Thomas, it has ceased to exist. Didn't you know that?'

'I didn't know that,' she flung back at him, surprised by her own sudden anger, afraid of it. 'I'm sorry,' she said.

And had she glanced up at that moment she would have seen him smile. 'Poor Miss Thomas,' he thought, 'she *is* upset.'

'Miss Thomas?'

She looked up, uncomfortably, shyly, 'Yes, Mr Blair?'

'Have you actually seen your brother following her about? Has he spoken to her, have they met on occasions?'

'He was once a *good* man, Mr Blair,' she said.

'He may not be the only one.'

She suddenly bowed her head; she felt as though she had been felled by an axe.

'Please,' she said, and again he felt his sleeve gripped, 'Please. You don't understand? It's not right. His chapel will empty.' Mr Blair sat bolt upright, fixed her with what might be the final stare, and said in the most casual way that she must really not upset herself like this.

'The Archbishop of Canterbury voted for private buggery, Miss Thomas, but his church has not yet fallen.'

She covered her face with both hands, bowed low, '*My* God!'

The doorbell rang again, the door opened and closed, the curtains moved, and then the assistant was bending over Miss Thomas.

'Are you all right, Madam?'

She saw that the woman had changed tables, noticed the spilt coffee.

'Are you all right? Would you like me to . . .' just as Miss Thomas's head came slowly up, she seemed not to see the assistant there, her eyes wandering about the room, and then she saw her. 'Er - - I - - what was - - -'

The assistant suddenly sat down by her, gave her a smile.

'I didn't know you knew Mr Blair,' she said. 'A very nice gentleman. He's regular here.' And after a pause, 'He's gone now, Madam,' but the words were gibberish in Miss Thomas's ears. She made to get up, but slipped back again.

'*Come* along . . .' and she felt an arm beneath her own. 'Come . . .'

But Miss Thomas didn't, and rose, and sat down again.

'I'll be all right in a moment, Miss,' she said. 'Leave me alone.'

'You don't look well, Madam, I'll get you the station cab.'

Miss Thomas cried quietly at the table.

'Poor thing.'

She got up abruptly. 'I'll get Mr Jenkins, the station,' she said. 'You really ought to go home.'

'I'm quite all right, thank you,' Miss Thomas said, struggled to her feet, clung to the table. She heard the girl on the telephone, who then returned, and said quietly, 'Sit down, Madam. He'll be here in a moment or two.'

They looked at each other, but said nothing, and there was much in the silence. She helped Miss Thomas into the cab, and she, so aware of the broad daylight and the main street of the town, bowed her head again, and thought of those that passed by, wholly unaware that the street at this moment was empty. Mr Jenkins looked at her. Mr Jenkins knew. He understood.

'Had a little faint the girl said. Not like you it isn't, Miss Thomas. You'll be all right tomorrow, course you will,' and he turned and smiled at the unsmiling passenger. A regular member of the Penuel chapel, Miss Thomas did not recognise him. She huddled in the back of the cab, longed to be home, alone in her room. Suddenly he stopped.

'Sure you're all right, Miss?'

She nodded, and it was enough for Jenkins, and they

drove on quickly to Ty Newdd. He helped her out, linked arms up the path.

'There now,' he said, giving her a sympathetic pat, 'that's it.'

And at last she smiled and said 'Thank you.'

'Home you are, always best in the end, Miss.'

He waited until she had got the key in the lock, opened the door and entered.

'Thank you.'

'Welcome,' he said, and drove back to the station, smiling all the way there, Miss Thomas being his first customer of the day. Margiad kicked back the door, and sighed with relief, made for the nearest chair, sat down.

'Terrible,' she thought, 'terrible,' remembering, with a kind of indefinable horror, the sight of the solicitor sitting at the table, so cool, so casual, almost indifferent to what she told him. 'And the things he said, the *things*.'

The words were new, she did not even understand the language that he spoke, in the strange climate of that empty cafe, the nightmare morning. She sat, still numbed, frozen into her experience, and was still sat, stiff and motionless, when, at twelve o'clock she heard the footsteps on the gravel and the key in the lock. She had not removed her outdoor things, and was sat with her back to him as he entered the room.

'Ah! There you are, Margiad,' he exclaimed in a cheery voice, but it only had chill for her, and she made no reply, but sat with her hands in her lap, and he saw the restless, twisting fingers. The fire that had gone down badly needed rousing, but she made no effort with it. He went into the hall, hung up his coat and hat, came back, and sat opposite her in the armchair.

'Well!' he said, 'here we are,' and settled back, and began feeling for his pipe.

'Margiad!'

She did not answer, and did not move.

'Are you going out?'

'I am not going out.'

He gave the fire a vigorous poke, and the flames came up. Almost jovially, he said, 'Well then, at least you can remove your hat, Margiad.'

She stared into the fire and remained silent.

He half rose, 'Why of course, what on earth am I thinking about, you've *been* out,' and he gave a curious little laugh.

He lit his pipe, spread legs, was suddenly comfortable.

'*Margiad!*'

He got up, leaned over her, 'Are you all right?'

'I am all right.'

'I saw old Miss Pugh,' he said, not seeing her, not wanting to, seeing only Miss Vaughan, thinking of Miss Vaughan, seeing her totally all the way from the hotel to her office door, and seeing no other, and wishing and hoping that for a single moment she might answer his good morning, turn, even smile, and he thought of another letter he had written her, he thought of tomorrow. If for a single moment she became *real*.

'Margiad!'

It seemed an age before she said in a hollow voice, 'Well?'

'The days have changed,' she thought, 'it's like becoming lost. My brother is a stranger to me, I do not know him.'

'Aren't you going to take off your things, sister?' he asked.

Slowly she began removing the pins from her hat.

He could not hide the sudden anxiety in his voice when he asked quietly, 'Are you not well, Margiad?'

She was miles from the room, from the sight of him, remembering only the waiting-room, a consulting room, the bespectacled Dr Hughes.

'Dr Hughes will not call,' she thought.

He extended a hand, 'Margiad?'

'How *is* Miss Pugh?' she asked, and so suddenly that it startled him.

'I told you, sister. I said she is well, and she *is* well. Live for years,' and more slowly, incisively, 'Didn't you hear me *say* that I had?'

'I don't know what you said,' Margiad replied, and went off into the hall and removed her coat and scarf and gloves. She stood there for a moment or two, undecided. Should she go up to her room, go straight into the kitchen, prepare the meal, as if nothing had happened. 'Did you give Miss Pugh my message?' she asked.

'Message?' and Mervyn came violently down from the clouds, and stuttered nervously, saying, 'Yes, of course, you don't suppose I'd forget, did you?'

'I don't know what you forget, and I don't know what you remember.'

She stood at the foot of the stairs.

'It's past noon, sister,' he said, feeling hungry.

'I did not notice the time,' she replied, and went slowly upstairs.

He got up, stood at the foot of the stairs, called, 'Margiad! Margiad!'

The bedroom door slammed in his face.

'Margiad,' he shouted. 'What on earth is the matter with you, sister?'

The door opened suddenly, she faced him.

'You won't starve,' she said. 'I shall be down in a minute.'

She did not sit down, she could not sit down, but stared out of the window.

'I shall not stay here.'

She closed the window, and opened it again. And then the salvo.

'He goes out at night. Where does he go? What is going on? What am I to do? Soon I will not be able to go to chapel myself.'

She heard him go into his study, slam the door.

'Let him wait,' she thought, and began idly wandering about the room, picking up first one object, and then another, thinking of other days, of acceptance and contentment, wishing herself back at Hengoed, wishing herself happy at Glan Ceirw, and one after another the pictures came, and she knew then that they should never have come to Garthmeilo, a miserable little town, a mean town. She heard him pacing his room, the door open and close again. 'Perhaps I'd better.' She gave a final glance through the window and went downstairs. Hearing her, he left his study, joining her in the kitchen.

'It's nearly one o'clock,' he said.

She was bent over the pans. 'Is it?'

'You can call me when it's ready,' he said roughly, and rushed back to his room.

'Ready now.'

They ate in silence, avoided each other's glances, wondering which would be the first to speak.

'Did you arrange with Price to collect Mr Richards's pension?'

'I did,' he said, and seemed to bend even lower over his plate.

'You were out very early this morning, Margiad.'

'I had things to do.'

'*What* things?'

She looked him squarely in the face. 'You make it sound like a criminal offence.'

'I'm sorry, Margiad.'

'And you have the right to be.'

'Will you stop interfering with my life.'

'I am only thinking of my own, Mervyn,' she replied, and helped herself to tea, and then quietly added, 'I thought of your life yesterday. Following this woman round like some little dog. You ought to be ashamed, at your age. Perfectly ridiculous.'

'Has the machinery of misery started up again?' he asked, and she thought he would get up and rush out of the room, but instead he went on eating, asked for more tea, and received it.

'Thank you, Margiad,' and later he said in a low voice, 'cannot one be even sorry for a creature?'

'Which creature?'

'There you go again,' he shouted.

'Don't shout at me, Mervyn,' and he saw the colour high in her cheeks.

'I am not *shouting*,' he cried, and shouted. 'Leave me alone.'

'I will leave the house.'

'Leave it then.'

He pushed his plate away, got up, and went to the fire and sat.

'You have changed Mervyn,' she said, and when he looked at her, he realised the deep hurt he had occasioned, and got up and went to her. 'Margiad, forgive me, I *am* sorry. Look at me, now, I say *look* at me,' and she looked, long and steadily, and then he said, 'What harm do I do?'

'That is a question I cannot answer.'

When the torrent came she drew away from him, but he gripped her arms, held her tight. 'Yes. I am in love with Miss Vaughan, I am, I knew it that first night she came to the chapel, I know it now, yes,' he continued through his teeth, 'I knew it then, *yes*, I do follow her about like a dog, and she neither looks nor speaks, but I know, I say I know I can make her happy. Lonely she is, I know that, too. And you know nothing, I mean nothing.'

'She is only in love with herself, Mervyn, I keep telling you that, and there's something queer about her, she has no friends, I told you that, too, but you believe nothing I tell you. The days are being torn to shreds, you are never in this house, you are seen, you are laughed at, they think you're mad, and that's the truth of it. And from what I hear she hasn't a penny, living in that awful room at Gandell's place, and why. Because she couldn't afford anything better.'

'*That*, doesn't matter to me.'

'Perhaps she's as mad as you are,' she flung at him.

'It doesn't matter.'

'She told that Mrs Gandell that her father went over a cliff at Tenby.'

99

His lips trembled, as he made to speak, but nothing came out.

'Perhaps she threw him over,' Margiad said. 'How do we know? We know nothing about her.'

'You went to Dr Hughes this morning, you went to talk about me, I expect you wagged your head off about your mad brother. Did you?'

She went into the hall, and searched about in her overcoat, came back with a small white box and handed it to him.

'Take two each night, Mervyn. They'll help you to sleep better. He said he might come and see you, though he seems to me such a very busy man that he might forget and not come at all.'

He looked at the box held out to him, and said, wildly, bewilderedly, 'What on earth is this?'

'Take it,' she said, and pushed the box nearer to him.

He tore it from her, opened it, and flung its contents into the fire. 'You've actually been spying on me, my own sister. It is I that am ashamed,' and he grabbed her again, shook her, and shouted, 'God Almighty. I am a grown man. I'll leave this house, I'll take lodgings in the town.'

'Take them.'

'I will stop preaching.'

'Then stop.'

'You know what you're saying to me?'

And she said very slowly, carefully, 'Yes . . . I do know.'

'Then you're no longer my sister,' he said.

'It will not stop you from becoming a fool,' she said.

The sudden break in his voice, the trembling lips, quite shocked her.

'Why are we doing this to each other, Margiad?' he asked.

'I wish I knew.'

'It simply cannot go on.'

'I know that, too,' she said, and got up, and left him, and left the house.

6

Jones had been sitting alone in The Lion for an hour now, and though there were three other men sitting about, they had not spoken to him, and it did not worry him. The licensee stood behind his counter and slowly polished the glasses. In The Lion Jones was known as Mrs Gandell's dog. And one after another the three men went out, but not without boisterous good nights to the man behind the counter.

'Night Tegid.'

'Night.'

And Jones, staring into the fire, heard the three separate slams of the door.

'Drinking slow this evening,' Tegid said, and put away the last of the glasses, but Jones appeared not to have heard, and sat quite still, the glass in his hand.

All the way to the pub the questions had nagged at Jones, circled round and round his brain. Was Miss Vaughan just imagining the whole thing? Had Mrs Gandell let him in? Would she do *anything* for money? The more he thought about it, the more certain he was that he had locked up that night. Tegid Hughes joined him, a glass of beer in his hand.

'You look thoughtful tonight, Jones' he said.

'Do I?'

'Yes,' and he gave him a cigarette, then lit his own.

'Thanks.'

'Done your duty then?' Tegid asked, and Jones grinned, and nodded. He had read her a whole chapter from *The Three Musketeers,* he had given her a cup of hot milk to help her sleep, told her he wouldn't be late. Her whole manner during the day had made him very nervous. Was she lying to him, was she planning to sell out?

'How are things?'

Jones at last looked up. 'Same as yesterday, the day before that, and the day before that one.'

'Think she'll make a go of it?' asked Tegid.

'*Yes.*'

'No need to bloody shout,' Tegid said.

'Sorry,' Jones said, 'ah, I'm always being sorry about something.'

'There's rumours about her, thinking of going . . . .'

'Rubbish!'

'Never paid even when the Owens had it,' Tegid said, 'wrong situation, too far away from the town, Jones.'

'She's all right,' Jones replied, and offered his glass, which Hughes took and went away and refilled.

'Here,' and pushed it into his hand. 'Got a mood on tonight then? Never opened your mouth since you came in.'

'Do I have to? How wide shall I open it?'

'OK, OK. It's a free country. Understood.'

And the sudden short laugh broke the chill in the air.

'Actually,' he continued, 'you've only had three people there since just after Christmas.'

'Telling me.'

'The one she's got now seems a queer sort of bird,' Tegid said.

'How queer?'

'Oh . . . people talk.'

'Go mad if they didn't, wouldn't they,' snapped Jones.

Tegid leaned very close to Jones, pressed hard on the Jones knee, and seemed to spit out the observation directly into his face.

'What've I ever done to offend you, Jones? And what haven't I done to *oblige* you both,' and he blew cigarette smoke into the other's face, and then he felt a hand on his knee.

'I was a bit upset today,' Jones said. 'Sorry again. Just forget it.'

'I might, and I might not,' Tegid said.

He saw the Jones glass suddenly empty, but did not take it, and went away and refilled his own.

'The three apostles kept their mouths shut,' Jones said, and drew on his cigarette.

'The *three apostles*?'

'They suffer from an excess of rectitude,' Jones said.

'You mean that lot that just went out?'

'That lot that just went out,' Jones replied.

'Still a free country, Jones.'

'And one of them was Pritchard.'

'That's right. He thinks you ought to marry Mrs Gandell. Not a bad idea either, considering,' and Jones immediately exploded.

'Considering *what*?'

Tegid gave a loud laugh, and replied, 'Everything, and a little bit more than that.'

He heard a call from an outer room, and called back, 'All right, Sarah, all right,' and a door slammed, and then Tegid leaned over Jones, took the glass and asked him to have one for the road.

'Thanks.'

'Welcome.'

'Having one yourself?'

'Yes.'

'Good,' Jones said, 'good.'

They drank each other's health, then, smiling a big smile, Tegid said in a low voice, 'I know what you've come for, Jones.'

'You *are* clever.'

And, offering still another smile, Tegid replied, 'And you may well think so, later.'

'Leave riddles where they belong.'

'Where do riddles belong then?'

And it came swiftly through Jones's teeth. 'To the Bards.'

And they both laughed. Tegid looked at his watch.

'Hardly any business at all today,' he said, 'and yet I feel kind of exhausted.'

'It's the way it goes.'

'I had that Glyn Prothero in here the other night. Talked about your place. Very damp,' he said, 'and the food wasn't up to much.'

'He said that? The swine. He was all smiles the day he left.'

'Only telling you what he said.'

'In the absence of anything else?'

Tegid chortled and replied, 'If you like,' and he again glanced at his watch.

'All right, all right, I got the message,' Jones said, huffily, banging his glass to the table.

'And they cost ninepence *each*,' Tegid said. He put a hand on the other's shoulders, saying, 'Didn't see you at chapel Sunday, Jones.'

'No.'

'That's changing, too, only about half a dozen people there, and not even his sister, Margiad.'

'He's suffering from a pain in his thighs,' Jones said, grinning.

'Thought there was something in it. They say he's following this bird about. That true?'

'What d'you think?'

'Asking you?'

'Think he'd like to get her in a dark corner.'

'Like *that*?'

Jones dropped his voice. 'Like that,' he said, and then very abruptly, 'Are you worried about it?'

'God! You have got a mood on this evening, Jones, you really have.'

'Gives me letters for her from time to time, and she throws them in the wastepaper basket, never even opens them.'

'Well? Just fancy that.'

It was almost worth just one more for the road.

'Give it me,' and Jones gave his glass. 'By the way, does your boss only give you the one night off a week?'

'She's not my boss,' Jones replied. 'And mind your own bloody business.'

'I do, but others don't, and that makes the split difference,' Tegid said, and handed him his final glass. He got up went to the door, opened it, and called out, 'Won't be long, Sarah, just locking up.'

'Get it down, Jones, and then I'm *pushing* you out. People who keep so much to themselves like your bird does, generally have money knotted away at the end of an old blanket, or even a pair of stockings.'

'That's her business.'

'I suppose it is.'

And at the top of his voice, Jones shouted, 'Of *course* it is.' Tegid put the flat of his hands on each Jones cheek, held him close, and said with a near hiss, 'Keep your hair on man.'

'Miss Vaughan's business is Miss Vaughan's business. She pays regularly for her board, and that's *our* business.' Jones replied.

'And now,' Tegid said slowly, as Jones got up, 'and now that something I mentioned earlier.'

'Oh yes,' and Jones was right on his toes. 'And what's that?'

'No more gin.'

'*No – more – gin?* Oh *hell!*'

'I mean it,' Tegid said.

'There were other places we could have gone to,' Jones said, 'but we came to you. Know why? Because you're decent.'

'One can be too decent, Jones.'

'Mrs Gandell always paid in the end, you know she did.'

'She doesn't give me my living. There are other people about.'

'So that's it.'

'That's it,' Tegid said.

'I can't believe it,' Jones said, and stared at him open-mouthed.

'Let you have a few cigarettes . . .'

But Jones had flopped back to his chair, too astonished to make a reply.

'She's had a lousy winter,' he said.

'We've all of us had a lousy winter.'

'You seem so bloody determined about it, Tegid,' and whispered, 'not the missus, is it?'

'I've always stretched a point for Mrs Gandell, but alas, Jones, the law of limitations comes into everything. Damn nuisance, but there it is. Cartref is not the only place struggling to make a living.'

And Jones rose again, stuttering wildly, 'I can't believe it, I *can't.*'

'I should though.'

He clutched Tegid's arm, and said slowly 'I can't go back without it, I can't . . . she . . . .'

'You had three bottles a week ago. Your boss should start trying having tea for her breakfast, Jones,' and he gave a slight laugh, and added, 'Makes a change.'

'You're quite determined.'

'I am. And I'm sorry about it, Jones.'

Quite involuntarily Jones cried out, 'What the hell am I going to *do*?'

Again the call came from an outer room, and Jones knew *she* was calling again. 'It's her,' he thought, 'been breathing down Tegid's neck, getting her teeth into it,' and it was all so real to Jones that he could even hear her whispering in her husband's ear, 'It can't go on, Tegid.'

'All *right*, Sarah, said I'm coming, didn't I?'

For the second time a door slammed loudly, echoed in the bar.

'What are you going to do, Jones? Tell you. *Beat* it.'

Parrot-like, Jones said, 'You really mean you won't?' and Tegid's gravely nodding head was the only answer he ever got.

'I *do*,' Tegid said, and put an arm under the Jones shoulder, walked him slowly to the door, and opened it wide. He looked up at the stars, heard the distant murmur of the sea.

'I don't understand,' and Jones continued to stare bewilderedly at this most obliging of licensees.

'Try not to then,' Tegid replied. 'I'll tell you two things before you depart, Jones,' and he put his mouth close to the Jones ear.

'That Glyn Prothero told me, in confidence, that Mrs Gandell's place won't last another three months . . . .'

'The bastard!'

And, stressing it, Tegid continued, 'And that Melvyn Pritchard that's just left this pub, you saw him sitting opposite you, well, he said something to me, and funny really, but somehow I can still hear the words in my ear,' and he took a tighter clutch on Jones. ' "When I look at that fellow, Jones," he said, "I look on a small, tight man to whom one says cringe, and he *cringes*, bend, and he *bends*, crawl, and he will *crawl*, hunch your shoulders, Jones, and he will *hunch* them. Jones smiles, Jones grins, but he never laughs, never. Jones is his own ten fingers and his mouth".'

Jones broke free.

'I never knew till now,' he said, 'that good people could be so disgusting.'

'Good *night*,' Tegid said, placed a knee under the Jones backside, and gave him a gentle push. 'And remember what I said, and remember what is owed to me.'

He closed the door and locked it, switched off the light, leaving Jones floundering in the darkness.

'The mean swine,' he thought, 'the mean . . .', and stood there, bent, his eyes closed. 'The things I used to do for him one time.' Rooted where he stood, staggered by sheer surprise: 'I'm not crawling to that bloody bank again, I *won't*,' resting on one foot, and then the other, and the words rocking in his ears, 'won't last three months.' Jones finally came erect, stiffened. 'Perhaps the bitch was lying to me this morning, perhaps she is planning to go. God, what'll I do if she does. Oh no, no. Who's lying,' and suddenly, and loud into the deserted road, 'Who's lying to me?'

He walked slowly, uncertainly on, into a darkness that appeared to deepen even as he strode, hands dug deep into his pockets, and at the corner of the next street, he stopped again, leaned against some railings, swaying a little, angry and bewildered. And he thought of the liar waiting, flat on her back, and he thought of the time, even heard that bosun's cry. 'That you, Jones?' As if it wouldn't be, tomorrow and the day after that, and Jones there, always ready. 'The lying *bitch*. She's pulling *out*.' The Jones world rocked under torrenting thoughts, and he turned a corner, walked on, heard the clear sharp bite of his own footsteps, stopping again, walking on, turning to look back, turning to go on, stopping again, staring up at the night sky, 'the bloody stars', and wondering, and wondering again, and wishing, and hoping. 'I never wanted anything else, *nothing*.'

From road to road, through street and street, and once, round and round again, and Jones lost, and empty, and floundering, and floundering again, and not a single answer for him in all that darkness and silence. And at last he stopped, looked up, and there was the Decent Hotel, and one single light still showing in an upper room. He gripped the railings, swayed a little, looking up again, at the squat building, and thought of the room, and the woman in it, waiting, waiting.

'The damned bitch. I can't believe it, I can't. Only this morning she said she wasn't even thinking of going, *swore* to it,' and the Jones effort induced a Jones belch. 'Ah, everything'll be all right soon as the bloody spring comes.'

He fumbled in pocket after pocket, searching for the key.

' "Late again, Jones," she'll say, "late again." And I won't give a *bugger* about it,' and he let go the railings and staggered up the path. He groped for the keyhole, found it, opened the door awkwardly and noisily and almost fell into the hall, and hung on to the still open door.

'That you, Jones?'

With some difficulty he managed to close the door, suddenly found himself on his knees at the foot of the stairs.

'*Jones*!' It sounded like a tocsin, reverberating through room after room.

'Yes' he cried, and it was more scream than shout. 'Jones is here.'

'You're late.'

He climbed half the stairs, then sat down, gave another belch, felt a draught on the stairs.

'Sorr - - - *ry*.'

'Are *you* coming *up*?'

'*Yes*.'

'Then come.'

She heard him, slow, and clumsy on the remaining stairs. She heard a bump, a creak of the floorboards, a surprising thud. 'Jones! You're drunk.'

'And so I bloody am,' he stuttered, and he rattled the doorknob, finally got a purchase and turned it violently, and the door fell in and he with it.

'You little swine, you said you wouldn't,' and Mrs Gandell leaned up on one elbow, glared at him, the words already forming acid on her tongue. 'You promised.'

Jones, swaying on the threshold stammered back, 'And so did you, you lying bitch,' and hurled himself into the room, leaving the door wide, reached bed, bent over it, over her, and she turned her face away.

He gripped both ends of her pillow.

'Tell me about it,' he said, and belched again.

'Tell you about what?' and she sat up, seemed on the point of hitting him, but changed her mind, and then he flopped heavily across the bed.

'You lied to me this morning, Mrs Gandell, you *lied* to . . . you . . .' but the remainder of his sentence died away in the bedclothes.

'Come along, Jones,' and she got up and began undressing him.

'Leave me alone,' and he pulled himself free, staggered across the room, and fell into the nearest chair.

She stood over him. 'You *promised*, Jones.'

'Ssh . . . .'

'*Come* along, Jones. I couldn't sleep, couldn't settle, I was worried about you, it's so late.'

The stream of gibberish that followed was quite beyond her. She undressed him where he sat, and when his head fell she propped it up again. 'You can be a bloody nuisance when you like, Jones.'

'This is all,' he stuttered, flung arms into the air, embraced the room. She raised him out of the chair.

'This is my home.'

'Come along now,' Mrs Gandell said, and Jones gave forth with another belch.

'This is where I *live*,' he said, as she slowly dragged him towards the bed, and finally flung him into it, then sat down.

'Sometimes you're positively silly,' she said, suddenly hating the Jones belch, the Jones breath. 'Over four hours, you said you'd be back by ten. It's getting on midnight,' but Jones, his face now turned to the wall appeared not to hear. She turned him over on his back, and he opened his eyes and looked up at her. She took a handkerchief and wiped his mouth. And fiercely, hotly into his ear. '*Jones*!'

She switched out the light, lay clear of him, listened to his heavy breathing; at any moment he would begin to snore.

'*Jones!*'

'What?'

'Where is it?'

'Where is *what*?'

'What I sent you for?'

She seemed to wait an age for the answer. 'He said *No*.'

'Who said no?'

'T - - t Tegid Hughes.'

'*Refused*?'

And Jones shouted, 'Said no.'

'Why?'

'Ask him, Mrs Gandell.'

She grabbed his shoulder, shook him. 'I'm asking *you*,' and she sat up and switched on the light, saw the Jones eyes closed, but the mouth wide open.

'You drunken swine.'

'S - - said you won't last three months, Mrs Gandell.'

'What the hell are you talking about?'

'Said you'd pull out.'

'Pull out?'

'Go,' shouted Jones, '*Go*, Mrs Gandell,' and slowly he raised himself up and lay over her, and felt neither wish nor warmth, the lie between them, 'and you - - - - you - - - you said you *wouldn't*.'

When he gripped her shoulders she broke free, and cried in his face 'Take that, you little bastard,' and struck him hard on the mouth. And like a duty to do, like a breath of the old times, she heard him stutter. 'Thank you, Mrs Gandell, th - - th - - -'

Her breath was warm at his cheek. 'You'll wake Miss Vaughan, Jones.'

'That Mr Prothero said it's lousy . . . he said . . . said . . .'

'What the hell are you talking about?' each word a hiss. 'What've you *done*, Jones?'

'My bloody duty,' he shouted.

'You'd better sleep it off. We'll talk about it in the morning.'

'*Morning*?' In a flash Jones exploded, and Jones was sober. 'Now,' he shouted in her face, '*Now*, Mrs Gandell,' and shook, and went on shaking her.

'Have you gone mad?' and again she struck him across the face.

'Thank you for that, I mean thank you *again*, Mrs Gan-

dell. I'm not crawling to your bloody bank, I'm not crawling to The Lion, I'm not crawling to *anybody*. I've had a
bloody nough.'

'Then get *out*.'

'Anything for cash,' he shouted in her face, 'I mean *anything*.'

And again he was too close, and she stared at Jones, his
face contorted with utter rage, and hated his breath and
the still occasional belch. She slowly drew up her leg, got
a foot into the middle of his back, and pushed. And Jones
was clear of the bed, flat on his back.

'Get out. *Now*.'

She got out of bed, knelt over him. 'I said get out. Now,
I mean now.'

'You let God's man in here the other night. How much
did he *pay* you, Mrs Gandell?'

'Let . . .' but the words died on her tongue.

'She - - - she *told* me.'

'Told you. *Who* told you?'

Jones came slowly into a sitting position, pushed her
away from him.

'The queer bitch next door that you love so much. How
much did he pay you to stand outside her bloody door?'
Then very slowly, 'and if you went to her room now I'd bet
you'd find her silly face in the stars. How *much*?'

'You had better begin packing your things, Jones,' Mrs
Gandell said, and got up and went to the bed, and sat on
it, and watched him, and waited. 'The difference between
us, Jones, is that you are dead drunk, and I'm sober.
Get up.'

But Jones made no move, felt suddenly rooted to the
floor.

'I'll get your things together myself, Jones,' and she got
up and began wildly opening drawers and cupboards, and,
as though the mad moments had passed, said quietly, 'and
always remember, Jones, that you can be done without.'

Jones fell flat on his face, and lay very still. She groped

in drawers and cupboards, and soon there lay a little pile of the Jones things.

'How *much*?'

But she did not hear, but now knelt and began to make a neat bundle of the Jones belongings.

'Mrs Gandell,' the words coming through spread fingers, hard up against the Jones mouth. 'Mrs Gandell?'

'I'm waiting,' she said.

'*Mrs* Gandell?'

She watched him come slowly to his knees, make to rise, fall again, make another desperate effort, and she went across and got him to his feet.

'There are your things, Jones. Now get out,' as he lay heavy against her, as he struggled to stand upright, as he pushed himself clear, staggered to the bed and lay stretched, hands to his mouth, and heard her say loud and clear that she meant what she said.

'You said you wouldn't *go*,' he blurted out, and she was startled by the sudden break in his voice, and the moment she sat on the bed he struggled into a sitting position, leaned against her, and muttered, 'You *said* it.'

'Said *what*, Jones?'

And Jones growled, 'What you said, that's all.'

She was aware in a moment of what was helpless, and what was craven in him, and the sudden fierce hug she gave him was that of mother to son. She got up, saying, 'I'm going to make some coffee, Jones. Get into bed.'

But his hands flopped to his knees, his head hung, and he did not hear her leave the room. When she returned he was in exactly the same position, except that the moment the door opened he looked up at her with such yearning that for a moment she thought he might even smile.

'Here! Drink this.'

'Thank you, Mrs Gandell.'

'You'll feel better in a minute,' she said, and sat close again, sipping her coffee.

'D'you know what, Mrs Gandell?'

'What?'

'All the way back from that pub I was thinking of my mother.'

'Were you?'

'Yes, I was,' and he finished the coffee and gave her the cup.

'Sometimes it's nice to remember, and sometimes it isn't,' she said.

'Know what she once said to me?'

'What did your mother say to you, Jones?' and she put an arm round his neck.

'You'll never be anything, she said.'

'*What* a thing to say.'

'So I was never anything, Mrs Gandell, that's how it is.'

'Dreadful, Jones, dreadful. How old were you then?'

'Fifteen.'

'Makes it even worse, Jones.'

'Doesn't matter now,' he said. She saw his trembling mouth.

'Where did you live?'

'In the mountains.'

'*Where?*'

'Doesn't matter,' Jones said. 'But you're not going to go, *are* you?'

'Of *course* not.'

'I never want to leave here, Mrs Gandell, *never*.'

'What happened after she said you'd never be anything, Jones?'

'Nothing. She went one way, and I went another, and whenever I came to a place I knew I'd do what I was told, and then I'd go on to another place, and it was the same there, and then I came here. Remember that. I carried your bags from the station. It was a very cold afternoon, the wind was East.'

'Fancy you remembering that,' she said.

'Sometimes I don't want to remember, Mrs Gandell.'

'Of course not, Jones.'

And at last she got him into bed, put away the tray, and

joined him. She switched out the light. They lay in the darkness, and for a few moments there was utter silence. He was restless beside her. She thought there were more words to come; she thought it would be better when they were free.

'Where is she now?'

'In another kingdom now, Mrs Gandell,' he said, and she knew that she could never say she was sorry.

'My mother used to write me twice a year, Jones,' very softly into the darkness.

'Did she?'

'Yes. But not now. She's very old, Jones.'

'Oh!'

'Eighty-five.'

'Think of that,' he said, and he came nearer, put a hand on her shoulder, and whispered, 'But you really won't go?'

'You must *believe* me, Jones.'

'Yes, Mrs Gandell. Sorry I was late.'

'Yesterday's Jones,' she thought, 'last week's, last month's.'

'Shall we forget it?' she asked. 'It's time we went to sleep.'

'If you left here, I wouldn't know what to do. Honest.'

'I am not leaving, Jones. I absolutely *swear* it.'

'The people *will* come.'

'Indeed they will.'

'And Mr Prothero and his friend will be here next week.'

'The ice is cracking, Jones. Remember, you always told me it would.'

'I remember.'

'I know you are lonely, Jones, I know what you are, I know what you want.'

'Thank you, Mrs Gandell,' he said, and she felt his lips about her neck. 'I'm so glad you're not leaving here, leaving me.'

And she sensed something helpless, even derelict, about the man beside her.

'Go to sleep.'

'Yes, Mrs Gandell,' and he turned over, and stretched, and lay quite still.

'What a strange, strange mixture he is,' she thought.

He suddenly mumbled something but it was quite incomprehensible to her.

'Poor Jones. Perhaps it was a mercy, Jones, that you never knew who your father was.'

'Perhaps, Mrs Gandell,' Jones said, 'perhaps,' and fell asleep.

She lay there, listening to the first gentle snores. She heard the clock strike two, the rain beat suddenly against the window. It was still February.

7

The bridge leading to the sea was quite deserted, and in the gathering dust of the evening nobody had noticed the man stood at the northern end of it, leaning on the rail, huddled in his overcoat, leaning heavily as from some quite recent exhaustion. And as he stood there he was aware that the discipline of his days, the very simplicity of his life, mocked him. He was aware that he had walked out of the silent house, but could not remember how long he had remained huddled over his desk, a sheet of paper crushed in his hands. He had come out to walk, to find a peaceful spot, to make a decision, and he could not. He thought again of the words on the paper, he read them, he felt them.

'Dear Miss Vaughan, there was once a woman that was careless in her years, and heeded not the words spoken unto her, and after a while she became sorely troubled by this, for in her country no vintage fell. Thus, a gathering never arrived to raise her up, and the land in her country came up with nought save briars and thorns.'

And he summoned the words in defence of his feelings. 'I harm none.'

'It is my life, *my* life.'

He turned his head to look south, and turned it again to look north. He was glad that he was alone. 'Should I – go away?'

And in a moment life was a darkness, chained to the ground. He defended and he doubted.

'I could marry her, we could be happy. *Why* not?' But Margiad was suddenly close again, the self-appointed life-belt, the final succour.

'She said that they opened my letters to her at the hotel, said they read them, and laughed at them.'

He imagined a hand on the Jones throat, pressing hard. 'What a place for her to live in.'

He knew that room, and the stairs to it; dream room, dream stairs. He thought of the Gandell woman, he loathed the Gandell woman, felt Jones's breath in his ear, heard the words. 'She draws pennies from stones.'

'I wish . . . .'

He walked slowly along the bridge, and when he came to the other end, stopped. The morning had returned to him, the waves of it, and suddenly he saw both women, struggling for a place beside him.

'I *am* lonely.'

Then he turned and made his way back to the house. Would she be there? Wouldn't she? He remembered the words of anger that had hit the ceiling. 'I am going,' Margiad said, and he heard the slam of the door, and then the silence.

Had she really gone? Deserted him. Not a soul passed him by, and he was glad of that. And there was Ty Newdd, and he thought of the study that was once peaceful, as he thought of the bridge he had just left, where of an evening his sister and he would sometimes stand and look out to the sea, watching the dying light.

The front door lay open just as he had left it, and now he longed to be in, dreading to be in.

'She wouldn't leave me. She couldn't.' He loved her, she was his sister, she was. 'She *can't*.'

He stepped into the hall and closed the door, removed hat and coat, glanced anxiously up the stairs, listening, wondering.

'Margiad! Are you there, sister?'

There was no answer. When he opened the sitting-room door the sight of the still bright fire was as welcoming arms to him. He crouched in front of it, warming hands that were blue and knotted with cold. He listened again, hoped again, and he pressed out the words. 'Are you there, Margiad?'

The silence un-nerved him. 'She *has* gone.'

He went upstairs, opened bedroom doors into empty rooms, then came down again. He sat down in his chair, made to pick up his pipe and light it, then suddenly exclaimed, 'No, of course not.'

He leaned to the fire again, rubbing his hands; there had been a kind of nakedness in the darkness outside that he was now glad to shed. He got up and opened the door, and called up the stairs. 'Margiad! Are you there, sister?'

There was no reply and he shut the door. Staring vacantly about the room he suddenly noticed that the window was closed, and went to open it. He had not drawn the curtains and the light from the room streamed down the garden. Something made him stand there, made him look out. And then he saw her, and his relief overwhelmed him. He opened the window and put his head out, wanting to cry, 'Margiad! Why there you are, you're still here. Thank God,' but the words remained locked on his tongue. He looked bewildered at this sight of her, her head turned away from the house, as though at this moment she was asking herself a question, still, in still air. His heart leapt, and he called out, 'Margiad! What on earth are you *do*ing there?'

And then he went out to her, and took her hand and pressed it. 'Margiad.'

She did not answer, she did not look at him, and the sound of his voice roused in her only a feeling of loathing and disgust.

'You'll catch your death of cold standing there, sister. Come along now. My God,' and he caught her in a fierce embrace. 'I'm glad you're here,' he said.

There was no response, and she had not moved. In his gentlest voice he said, 'Do come along, Margiad, *do* come into the house,' and he led her back up the path, and they paused for a moment on the step. 'I really thought you'd deserted me.'

He took refuge behind the words that were normal.

'*Come* along, I went for a walk myself, just got back.'

She would not look at him, and then he realised she had freed her hand from his own. They went inside, stood in the hall, faced each other in a confusing silence. He led her into the sitting-room. 'There,' he said, 'there, Margiad.'

He brought her to the fire, made her comfortable, and she sat stiffly, awkwardly, as though this house and this room and this chair were strange to her. He leaned over her. 'How long have you been standing out there, sister?'

She turned her head to the fire, and said quietly, 'I didn't notice.'

'Could have caught your death of cold out there, Margiad.'

He offered a smile, saying, 'I'll go and make a pot of tea.'

'Don't bother.'

'I *want* to,' he said.

She remained silent, and he went off to the kitchen. When later he returned with two cups, and handed her one, she shook her head, and he took it back to the kitchen again. When she looked at him she knew that he was looking, not at her, but through the open window of his own relief. And here he was, back again, sitting opposite her, casually stirring his tea, as though nothing in the world had ever happened, no single blow from anywhere against the peace of the day. His very calmness disturbed her, and once he even essayed a smile. But suppose she had *not* come back. Suppose she *had* gone off to Hengoed, and stayed there. Shyly, tentatively, he looked at her, and said in a low voice, 'Margiad! Margiad!' but it only prompted her to immediate action, and she picked up her work basket, and began rummaging through its contents.

'You really - - - are - - - angry, sister,' he said. The needles began to click, he watched the fingers that were lively, grow livelier still.

'How very calm she is,' he thought, and after a while, the silence angered him; it seemed to hold in it both teeth and gall.

'*Margiad!*'

She ignored him. He simply was not there. She heard his cup sound on the hearth, heard the match struck, and felt the room fill with the shag smell.

'I shall go to my study,' Mervyn said, not going, not wanting to, dreading a move, as he sat, as he watched the busy, but now infuriating fingers, that seemed to spell an indifference across the whole room. He contemplated upon the stiffness with which she sat, and the downcast head. His voice seemed strangulated as he asked, 'Are you never going to say anything to me, sister.' And again waited, again hoped. 'Shall I say it for you?' She turned her head away, she would not answer. And then he was stood over her. 'I am suddenly a man, and you call it a sin.'

The moment she looked at him he lowered his eyes.

'Where do you go at night?' she asked.

'*Where* do I go at night? I go out for a walk.'

'Walk?'

'*Walk*,' he said, 'I go for a walk, and I think about my life.'

'What about your life?' and he felt the harshness in the words.

He leaned even closer, and heaved it out, angrily, passionately, 'It's *empty*.'

'It won't stop you from becoming a fool,' she said, 'and nobody from laughing.'

'I don't - - - *care*.'

She dropped the knitting, spat it in his face. 'I *do*.'

She felt his fingers on her knees, felt them pressing down.

'Your respectability turns good intention into *slime*,' he said. There was a long silence, and they stared each other out.

'Mervyn Thomas, I will never forgive you for that. *Never*.'

'Then *don't*,' he shouted in her face, 'Don't,' and rushed back to his chair and huddled in it, closing his eyes, refusing to listen, refusing to look, heard her returning her things to the work basket. When the heavy sigh came his shoulders slumped; the moment had brought its cringe. He heard her get up and cross the room, heard her fiddling with the window catch.

'I stood out there,' she said, 'thinking of how peaceful and good our life once was. It is a great pity, Mervyn, a great pity.'

He spoke in such a low voice that she had to strain her ears for the words, as he said with a complete calm, 'I would marry Miss Vaughan tomorrow, Margiad. Is that a crime?'

'She *is* married.'

He gave a violent jerk in the chair. '*Is* married?'

'Is married,' Margiad said.

'To *who*?'

'To herself. She loves herself.'

'What on earth are you talking about, sister?' and she knew he was right behind her. 'What do you mean by *that*?'

'Ask Mr Blair,' she said.

'Mr *Blair*?'

'Mr Blair,' she said. 'I saw him this morning.'

'You - - you - - you seem to have been seeing everyone on my behalf.'

'I was having a cup of coffee in a cafe, and he was there. That's all.'

He turned her violently round. 'You're enjoying this,' he said. 'What right have you to interfere with my life?'

'I have to think of my own,' she said.

She broke free of him. 'Leave me *alone*. I am going to my room,' and she pushed him away and hurried to the door. He followed her out, followed her up the stairs. There was something he wanted to say, and he did not say it, something he wanted to do, and he did not do it. He opened the bedroom door for her, went in behind her. She had gone quite pale, her shoulders heaved, she sat heavily on the bed. He sat beside her.

'Margiad!'

'Go away,' she said, and he went away.

The study door slammed, the house was silent again. Slowly she got up and walked to her dressing-table, and sat down in front of the mirror, staring into this for a long time, and seeing nought save this brother that had changed so violently, heard the laughter that he did not hear. 'Poor Mervyn. Poor brother.'

She took out a handkerchief and wiped her eyes. When she opened them again the man in the mirror had vanished, and she saw only the days and places that had once been their peace. Why had they ever come to the town, and suddenly she was hating it, and everything in it. 'If he had stayed at Hengoed he would be deacon now.' She thought of Vaughan, she hated Vaughan. 'Living in the clouds, like she is.' If only they could both get up and go away, now, this very minute. Yes, if only they could. Mervyn was really a good man at heart. Her thoughts ran riot. He was so *obsessed* with this woman, so secret, hiding away from others. Hiding from what? And she thought of Tenby and her father over a cliff. When she thought of the morning she covered her face with her hands, and she saw the world raw behind her brother's broad back. She went to the door and called loudly, 'Mervyn!'

And he called back from the bottom of the stairs, 'What is it, sister?'

'I think I'll go to bed.'

'*Now*?'

'Now.'

'Wait a minute, I'm coming.'

She was still seated before the mirror when he came in.

'What is the matter?'

He stood just inside the door, and she said, 'Come here, Mervyn,' and he came. He sat down beside her, wanted to, but did not take her hand.

'You hate me,' she said.

'*Hate* you?'

'Because I am decent, and you are not.'

'I don't hate you, I don't hate anyone. Fancy saying such a thing to me, Margiad.'

'I listened to people this morning and I didn't even understand their language,' she said.

A rash moment, rash words, and he could no longer help himself.

'Perhaps they did not understand yours,' he said.

'You are brazen.'

'You're becoming impossible, Margiad.'

'These past weeks I've asked myself how on earth you can sit in your study and write the things that you do. The flowers of flesh grow in your skull, Mervyn.'

'We're *all* flesh. It's a prison.'

'Come and look at yourself in this mirror, you stupid man, look slowly and carefully. Spell your *age*.'

'Leave me *alone*.'

'You are left alone.'

'I'll meet her one day. You *see*.'

'You *are* mad.'

'I'm what I am,' and he closed his eyes for a moment. 'You appear to have seen a number of people on my behalf.'

There was no reply.

Suddenly he felt her hand warm on his own.

'Will you promise me, brother, to give it all up? Forget it.'

She moved away, and then he heard her at the window, fiddling with the catch. 'You don't even know you're ill, Mervyn.'

'For God's sake leave me alone,' he cried.

'You were once an upright man,' she said.

He sat on the stool, twiddled his fingers.

'Sordid,' she shouted, 'Sordid. Even the place she stays at is sordid. Not even a carpet on the stairs. There *are* other places. Quite obviously she hasn't any money, and that Mr Blair pays her starvation wages. God alone knows what she did at Dinbych.'

He got up, went to the window. 'Dinbych? I thought she came from Melin.'

'Dinbych,' Margiad replied. 'She answered Mr Blair's advert in a paper there. And what was her father doing at Tenby? To fall over a cliff there?'

'You're a real crusader,' he said, 'I can even see the lifebelt in your hands, Margiad.'

'Go away,' she said.

He stood beside her, and when she looked at him she enjoyed the moment of his helplessness. 'You are even beginning to *look* like a fool, Mervyn. Now leave me alone.'

'You wouldn't go, Margiad, you wouldn't just *go*.'

'I said leave me *alone*.'

She heard the door close, the creak on the stairs. And then she began to pack. She took two suitcases from the wardrobe and laid them on the bed. Then she went to the chest of drawers and began to sort out her belongings. From time to time she took a dress to the light, and carefully studied it, then folded and put it away. She felt intensely sad, and once stood over the half filled case, staring at the contents, the moment made real when she looked at the open wardrobe, the pulled out drawers.

'He can make an exhibition of himself if he wishes, but I'll not stay here,' and she thought of her last visit to Penuel, heard the tittering of the woman behind her, heard her brother called a silly old man. She thought of him now, back in his study, dreaming his mad dream about a woman that lived in the clouds. Shameful. Awful. 'Perhaps he'll deliver her another letter, and she'll toss it into the basket,' and that night Jones would read it aloud as he lay with the English bitch, and they would laugh, and she could hear them laughing. She finished her packing, and pushed the cases under the bed, after which she sat in the chair, and cried quietly to herself. Once, they had been happy, had lived for each other; once they held high their heads and were respected, and now . . . and she wiped her eyes. She would go to her sister. She would not return to the house. She went and lay on the bed, suddenly stiffened there, appalled by her own decision.

'We are simple people, and there is a way for us,' she thought.

The silence of the house was so intense that when her brother began to pace his study, the steps came up loud and clear to her.

'After all these years,' and she saw him, a good man, falling to pieces.

The pacing continued, and it did not stop, and the words followed behind him, out of his sister's mouth, and they would not let him alone.

'One fine morning you'll lose your chapel.'

'You are *ill*.'

'You'll feel the root go.'

'You annoy me by your silliness. Wake up. Your years are crags, and they will never be velvet. Grow up, Mervyn.'

He stopped dead in his tracks, and thought, 'Perhaps I *am* ill. What'll I do?'

He returned to his desk, covered his head with his hands. After a while he sat up, looked out at the surrounding darkness, got up and closed the windows, switched out the light, and sat still in the darkened room. The world diminished, and then he heard the footsteps in his head, as Miss Vaughan walked on, sublimely indifferent to one that thought her lonely. He remembered the first evening he had seen her, and saw her now, small, and quiet, and still, seeming so separate from others that sang when he sang, and she listened, and he watched her listen, and suddenly look his way, and he was lost in a moment, the words confusing on his tongue, until quite suddenly he murmured before an astonished congregation, 'My God,' then, after a pause, found his peace again, and then began his sermon. But Miss Vaughan was no longer there. She had vanished.

'I'm in love with her,' and she was in the room, filling, drenching it.

'I know I could make her happy.'

And suddenly Miss Vaughan was pushed rudely from his sight, and his sister was there, barring the way.

'Gone,' he said, and dropped his hands to the desk, thought of his sister's life, his own. 'If she answered one single letter, if . . . .'

He left the study and returned to the sitting-room, he put coal to the fire, he sat down, lit his pipe, and lay back. The door opened and Margiad came in, went straight to her chair and sat down. For an awful moment he thought she would renew her frantic knitting, instead of which she sat quietly and looked to the fire. He looked at his watch.

'Supper, Margiad,' he said, and immediately she left the room.

If only he could find a way in, by one single word. He listened to the kitchen noises, the tap tap of her restless feet, the shattering sound of a falling pan, and he called loudly, 'Can I help?' There was no answer. She came in and laid the table. 'Can I do anything?'

'Nothing,' she said, 'nothing.'

'*Very* well,' dragged from the tongue, pained, irritable, he wanted to shout in her face, 'Let there be an *end* to it.'

She came in, they both sat down, she served him, he began to eat.

'Margiad! *Please.*'

'Not again,' she replied, and went on with her supper.

'I wish,' he began, 'I wish that . . .' but she wasn't listening.

'I know how you are feeling,' she said.

'Your good intentions have wings, sister.'

'I worry about you because you are my brother, Mervyn, and I hide my head in the town more often than I do not.'

'The lifebelt shines in your eyes,' he replied, and gave a curious little laugh.

'She has no friends, and wants no friends, she likes what she is, what she does. She loves herself, Mervyn. Miss Vaughan is her own business.'

'She seems to be yours,' he shouted in her face.

'You don't even see what is happening,' she said.

'For God's *sake*.'

'You know there would be a living for you at Hengoed. Can't you think about it, can't you make up your mind, Mervyn?'

He got up and returned to the fire, relit his pipe.

She got up, began clearing the table, and said casually, 'He laughed then.'

'Who laughed?'

'Mr Blair.'

'Mr *Blair*?'

'*He* knows all about your following that woman about. I told him straight out how worried I was about you, and he laughed *again*.'

'Laughed *again*?'

She was suddenly so close to him that he drew back as the words came from between her teeth. 'I only said that I thought you would be left with an empty chapel. It was horrible, the way he smiled at me and said that the Archbishop of Canterbury had once voted for private buggery in the House of Lords, but it did not follow that the church had fallen. "Nor will your brother's chapel empty," he said.'

'Margiad!'

'*Buggery*,' she shouted in his face. 'That's the world, Mervyn, the *world*.'

He followed her to the door. 'You *are* upset,' he said, 'I'm sorry, Margiad, I'm ...'

'Leave me alone,' she said, and banged the door in his face.

He leaned heavily against the closed door; he thought to himself. 'Perhaps she is right. Perhaps I am going mad.' And he went upstairs, knocked on her door, and receiving no answer opened it.

'Margiad! Please speak to me.'

She had gone to bed. 'Margiad!'

Her finger went to the light switch. 'Don't speak to me.'

'I must,' and he went and stood over her. 'I cannot help myself.'

'Go away.'

But he stood there, speechless, aware only of a feeling of emptiness all about him, and suddenly she turned her face to the wall.

'Please,' he said, '*please*.'

'Go away.'

'Listen . . . .'

'I have,' she said.

'Try to understand *my* feelings,' he said.

'I have done my best. Soon I will not be able to leave this house.'

'I mean no harm to anybody, Margiad' he said.

She turned over, stared at him. 'You throw your duty into the gutter,' and then he sat down on the edge of the bed.

'Nothing is simple, Margiad, nothing.'

'People are talking about you.'

'I don't hear them.'

'You're stupid, blind,' she said.

She felt his hand on her shoulder, she shrugged it away.

'The first time I saw her in the chapel,' he began, and she sat up, suddenly smiled in his face, and said, 'I expect she'll marry the Colonel.'

The expression on his face shocked her, and he got up, made as if to speak, and didn't, then stuttered it slowly out, 'Colonel? What Colonel, *what* . . . .' stumbled across the room and collapsed in the chair. He went quite limp.

'Mervyn!'

His head drooped lower still, 'Oh no, not that, not that.'

In a moment she was stood over him, but he did not see her, and she never realised the blow she had struck.

'I'm sorry, brother, I am, I *am*,' leaning over him, clutching him, 'Mervyn, *Mervyn*.'

'I can't believe it, I can't,' and she could not close her ear to that sudden break in his voice.

She threw her arms round him, held him tight, 'Mervyn, Mervyn.'

'Colonel, Colonel - - - what Colonel, *what* Colonel?'

She hated this, she hated the sight of him there, mumbling the words, trembling visibly, and suddenly shouted in his face, 'You are not the only one that is lonely.'

And to break the following silence repeated it in an even louder, angrier voice. 'You are not.'

He caught her hands, suddenly realised she was there, close.

'What Colonel, Margiad?'

'I did not ask her.'

Defeated, angry, humiliated, he said, 'Who?'

'*Her.*'

'Is that the truth, sister?'

'I do not lie to you.'

Margiad seemed no longer there, even her voice seemed distant.

'There was only one Colonel ever in these parts, and he used to live at a place called Y Briach. But he's been dead for years.'

'I said you're not the only one that is *lonely,*' and screamed it in his face.

'Is this *true*?'

Her own casualness surprised her. 'I understand they have lunch together once a week.'

'I don't understand.'

'I thought you wouldn't,' she replied. 'You understand so little.'

'But . . . .'

The words were knives. 'But what?'

'Nothing,' he said, his voice fading, 'Nothing.'

'You had better go,' she said, 'I want to go to bed.'

He sat up, half rose, and exclaimed in a loud voice, 'I can't believe it, I can't.'

'Then don't,' and left him sitting there and went back to bed.

'I shall put out the light,' she said. 'You had better go.'

'It's impossible, imp*oss* . . . .'

'You should ask your friend, Jones who works at that

horrible hotel.'

'He is not my friend.'

'You've been seen talking to him on occasion, right out-side the place. Perhaps you were only enquiring the time of day.'

He got up, walked slowly to the door. 'This has been the most terrible day,' he said.

'She won't always be there, Mervyn.'

'We seem hardly like brother and sister,' he said.

'Perhaps we are not.'

He immediately closed the door, returned to the bed, removed her hand from the switch, and sat down. 'Margiad?'

'Well?'

'Why are we tormenting each other like this?'

'If that hotel lasts another three months, only Mrs Gan-dell and that lickspittle of hers will be surprised.'

He knelt down, he tried to take the hand that she withdrew.

'You wouldn't really go, Margiad, leave me, *now*? You wouldn't.'

'Don't make an exhibition of yourself,' she said.

Again his hand was reaching for her own, and again she pulled it back.

'Believe me, Margiad, I am genuinely in love with Miss Vaughan. Believe that.'

She flung it back at him. 'And the world knows. We are both being laughed at. You are mad, Mervyn, you *are*.'

'How bitter you are.'

'You think of nobody but yourself, you're selfish, *selfish*. I have feelings, too, Mervyn.'

He threw himself across the bed. 'I wish I was *dead*.'

'That is being *too* simple.'

His very inertness, the dead silence, disgusted her, and she said again, 'I have feelings, too, Mervyn. *Me*. Your sister that has lived a lifetime with you.'

He felt her hand at his shoulder, and all too surprisingly

her fingers in his hair, and he knew he had never been so close to her as this.

'Let's leave this place, Mervyn, let's go back where we were happy and peaceful. I've come to hate this place, and everything in it,' and she went on stroking his hair. 'Please,' she said, 'please.'

'You ask too much.'

'Nobody calls here now,' Margiad said. 'But I hardly think you'd notice that.'

The words sprang to his lips, but he never spoke them.

'Nobody writes,' Margiad said.

'She is too good,' he thought, 'too good.'

'The mornings are so empty,' she said. 'It was so different once. People that depended on you, waited, and you always came. They used to come to this very house, and you talked to them in your study, and you helped them, and they looked up to you. There are some things that are nice to remember. And only yesterday I had positively to *beg* you to call on old Miss Pugh. They are good, simple people, Mervyn, and they do not understand. Now you just sit in your study, hour after hour, day after day.' She gave a faint sigh, and continued. 'It's worse at night. I lie here thinking about it. The house has no warmth, no meaning any more. Sat in the dark when you should be in your bed. There are times, Mervyn, when you don't even appear to realise that I am here, *me*, your sister. Oh God! I wish I could help you.'

He drew back, sat up, then abruptly got to his feet.

'I understand all that you are saying to me, Margiad, but I have no answer for you.'

'If you haven't an answer perhaps you have a question?'

'Leave me alone,' he said.

As he turned away she got out of bed and followed him to the door. 'Look at me,' and he looked at her.

'Well?'

'If your father were alive today, I should be sorry for him. Go away and hug your silly dream. One day I shall laugh at you myself,' and she pushed him out of the room, and leaned all her weight against the door as she closed it, and the room was full of the fallen words. 'I've been his crutch for a lifetime,' she thought, and got back into bed and switched out the light. She heard him close downstairs windows, heard the bolt shot back on the front door, heard him come upstairs, his bedroom door close. There was nothing more that she could do, nothing more that she wanted to do, and he would get her answer tomorrow. Had he gone to bed? Was he standing at the window, staring out? Was he even thinking of going out again? Was he sat in his chair thinking of her, someone that he had never spoken to? She closed her eyes, she was glad the day had come to an end. 'Twenty years ago, ten - - - but now - - - -'

She thought of their brother, if only he were here, but he was oceans away. 'Something has come to an end,' she said. She got out of bed, knelt down, and prayed for Mervyn, and even the sound of a heavy thud in his room did not disturb her.

'I will go tomorrow,' she thought, 'yes, I will go tomorrow,' she said and got back into bed. Lying there, she was suddenly aware of a stillness, the very silence of the house, the calm sea after the wreck of the day. She buried her head under the sheet, she could not think of tomorrow. It seemed already torn in two.

In the next room her brother was sat in his chair, facing the wide open window, the blackness within as one with the blackness without. And he heard nothing save the distant murmur of the sea.

8

Garthmeilo opened its eyes to another day. The wind had
died down. Even the rain had ceased, though watchful eyes
scanned the sky, the still scudding clouds. This was the
ritual of the morning. Jones was up promptly at half past
six, remembering nothing of the night before. Mrs Gandell
rose heavily at half past seven. And at half past eight Miss
Vaughan came down to breakfast. Under the dim dining-
room light she heard the terribly used words of yesterday
circling the room, their echoes following. And Mrs Gandell
put on the smile that seemed to survive the voyage from
one empty day to another. Had Miss Vaughan slept well?
Yes, Miss Vaughan had slept very well. Good. Splendid.
The exchanges shot over Jones's head as he served her in
utter silence. Perhaps Jones had not slept well, and once
or twice he caught Miss Vaughan staring at him. Later, out
of a corner of her eye she watched them eat in silence. They,
in turn, watched her at her breakfast, and having finished
it, attend to the morning ritual, spectacle cleaning, powdering her nose, examining herself in the tiny mirror, after
which she got up and left the room in which only the
sound of eating could now be heard. They heard the outer
door close. Miss Vaughan had gone off into the world
again. Sometimes Garthmeilo watched, and sometimes
waited. Curtains moved, and once or twice a shopkeeper
took an unusual interest in his own window. They watched
her go by, her short sharp steps ringing out on the pavement, her bag tight under her arm, the other swinging
vigorously as she drew nearer and nearer to the round of
her new day, her head in the air, her purpose resolute and
unchanging.

'Here she comes.'

'There she is.'

'They say Thomas's sister has left him.'

'Well indeed No? Did she really then?'

'Terrible row they had, they say she's off to Glan Ceirw where they used to live.'

'Think of that.'

'I saw him yesterday. Ill he looked. Poor man.'

And back at the hotel Mrs Gandell was precise, and as sure as Jones himself was uncertain.

'The basin in number one is cracked, Jones. Have you noticed it?'

'Yes.'

'And those sheets in number two are quite worn, and must be replaced. I think you'd better go into the town and get new ones from Davies.'

'Yes,' Jones said, slowly coming clear, being aware, and quite suddenly attentive. 'The same kind of sheet, Mrs Gandell?'

'Of *course*,' she snapped.

'Right.'

'And clear these things away, Jones,' she said, and went away to her office.

'Certainly, Mrs Gandell,' and Jones piled the tray and went off to the kitchen. He hoped the day would go well, he hoped she wasn't going to have another mood, wasn't going to preach at him about being so late, coming back empty-handed. Mrs Gandell was far too occupied even to remember the night before, her morning had turned out to be as sharp as a razor blade, the unexpected having turned up, right out of the blue. Sat in her office, mountainous over her ledger, she could hear Jones busy in the kitchen. The pages of the ledger she turned ceaselessly to and fro, as she read, as she remembered. The Decent Hotel had actually had its good days. Her eye would suddenly light on a name, a date, and it buoyed her up. Backwards and forwards she went, always perusing, remembering, sometimes smiling. Yes, there had been some good times at the hotel.

All was not yet lost. Day dreaming. It helped to rid her mind of a quite leaden moment, when, coming downstairs she had found the letter under the door, and was still glad that Jones had not got there first. This letter, unopened, she had hastily thrust into the ledger, where it still lay hidden between the last two pages. She was mindful of this, it must not accidentally fall out, with Jones in sight. She had not expected it. She had not wanted it. The name of the sender was in bold black on the flap, and it sent a slither of ice down the Gandell spine. Midland Bank. Why open it? Why *read*? She had had them before. There was a neat little pile upstairs, safe in the locked draw of her bureau. She knew the message inside it, it seared her mind. And again she breathed a sigh of relief that Jones had not seen it.

'I suppose I shall have to go and see him.'

She heard Jones open the front door, got up and followed him out.

'*All* the windows, Jones,' she said, as she watched him prop up the ladder, and begin to ascend with his bucket. 'But be careful.'

'Will be careful, Mrs Gandell,' Jones said, and reached the top.

'How long?' she asked.

He looked down at her and replied, 'Three hours, I'd say, since you want them all cleaned.'

She called up, 'The whole place must be cleaned out, Jones. We'll do it after lunch.'

'Very well,' and then she went back to the office, and the ledger. She thought of the bank, she couldn't stop thinking about it. Only the fact that two guests were arriving in a few days' time, lightened the moment. She took out the letter, opened it, and read: 'Dear Mrs Gandell, Going through your account yesterday, it occurred to me that it might be a good opportunity for us to meet again, and perhaps to our mutual advantage. I would suggest Friday morning about ten o'clock. Please write and confirm, or telephone, if you must. Yours faithfully, Cledwyn Griffith.'

'If you must.' The three words sounded like threats. She crushed the letter into a tiny ball, and thrust it deep into the pocket of her overall. 'I haven't seen Griffith in a whole year.' But her ambassador extraordinary, Jones, had done his duty there some six months previous. It made her remember so clearly that she could already see Mr Griffith's very comfortable office, with its big mahogany desk, and the thick red carpet. She even saw the cigar box, though he only filled his office with their splendid aroma, for very special clients. She closed the ledger, went to the kitchen, and there dropped the letter into the stove, after which she went upstairs, opened the top drawer of the bureau, and took out four letters from the bank, marked Private. They were still unopened. On Friday she would remember them all the way to the bank, lead to her feet. She couldn't ask Jones again, daren't.

'God Almighty! Why did it have to come today, of all days. I *can't* be in the red again, I simply can't.' She picked up the calendar on the bureau, studied it, exclaimed, 'Thank God.' Forty-eight hours would kill February, and the sun must be somewhere around, and it was. She could see it now, shining on hillside and mountain, hear the singing water in the streams, hear the march of feet from England. She went to the cupboard and helped herself to a glass of gin, lit a cigarette, sat back in her chair, and made an imaginary voyage into the days that were warm, and the light bright. Even the sound of those distant voices was sudden music to her. Sometimes she had despaired, sometimes decided to go, to give it all up, but now, no, not now. The thoughts were already lessening the distance to the bank, even bringing a faint smile from Mr Griffith's thin face, she could actually see him smiling. And she smiled herself, puffed vigorously at her cigarette, enjoyed her slow sipping of the gin. When the clock struck half past eleven she got up and went downstairs to inspect the results of Jones's industrious endeavour. He was still at the top of the ladder, busy on the corner windows when she went out.

'Nearly finished, Jones?'

Jones was very definite. 'Quite finished, Mrs Gandell,' and came slowly down the ladder, put down the bucket and drew back to pavement edge, and looked up. He even offered her a smile.

'Shining like eyes, Mrs Gandell. Lovely.'

'I'll be in the dining-room,' she said.

'Yes, Mrs Gandell,' and Jones departed dutifully with ladder and bucket and cloths.

'I thought he'd never get done. Haven't been done for months.' She reminded him of this when he came in.

'And the bloody rain hammering them night and day for the past month, Mrs Gandell. What a waste of energy.'

'You can have a drink, Jones,' she said, and he followed her upstairs.

'Ah!' he exclaimed, 'Ah! Totally unexpected, makes the morning change colour.'

She flung him a cigarette. 'First of March Friday,' she said.

Jones clapped hands, cried, 'Hurrah!' then wished her good health.

'And think of it. Mr Prothero and friend coming at the weekend.'

Jones hurrahed again, it was like fireworks, gay lights, all the days before kicked into the sea and forgotten.

'You've been so patient, Mrs Gandell,' he said. '*So* patient.'

'I want to talk to you about some idea I have, Jones,' she said, and he sat forward at once.

'Yes, Mrs Gandell?'

She finished her drink, got up, and said, 'Come along now,' and Jones did his duty and came along, and they went from one room to the other. 'I'd like to have new wallpaper in both those rooms, Jones.'

'I know' he said, dragging it, and wondered 'when, how?'

They came to Miss Vaughan's attic room. She opened

138

the door, but did not step inside. Jones smiled, and stepped in.

'Holy of Holies,' he said. And then she followed him in.

There was a large book lying open on the bed, and she picked it up and studied it, idling through the pages, pausing to look at an illustration or two.

'What is this?'

'Welsh,' he said.

'But what *is* it?'

'Mabinogion,' Jones said, and took it from her, and glanced at the opened pages.

'Oh.'

'Fairy tales,' he said, 'and if you happen to like that sort of thing, very nice indeed. *Very* nice.'

'Children?' asked Mrs Gandell.

'Grown-up children also, Mrs Gandell.'

'Have you read it, Jones?'

'Yes.'

She walked out, and Jones closed the door after him. And then back to their own room, the ugly furniture, the wallpaper and the sad faded birds and flowers; back to the tight, unchanging life of this room, in which both of them felt safe, secure, close, bound. They shared everything with each other. They shared the winter, the ritual of their ordinary days. Jones rose at the exact time each morning, and, after hasty ablutions rushed down to make the early morning tea, made the usual inspection of the dining-room, carefully examining the tables. There were no crumbs, and nobody had stolen anything. Whilst the kettle sang he went and collected the morning papers, and any mail that lay under the door. Mrs Gandell received little mail, and Jones always went carefully through it, just in case. But there was never any letter for him, and he was never disappointed. Christmas was the exception when Mrs Gandell would send him a card. He appreciated that. Having made the tea he went upstairs and served Mrs Gandell, and then himself.

After which the curtains were drawn, a cursory glance at the morning sky, and then the morning paper, which neither of them ever read. Mrs Gandell lay back in bed whilst Jones opened the paper, rushed through all the headlines until he came to the page where the day's fortunes were told. He would then read out her fortune for that day, and then his own. The paper was then folded up and added to the fire kindling pile. He then switched on the transistor and they listened to the weather forecast, and after that, the news. They never discussed the news. He took the transistor down and put it on the sideboard, where it remained for the convenience of any guest. Miss Vaughan had not, to date, made any request to listen to either the weather or the news. Miss Vaughan, living inside Miss Vaughan, liked it that way, and she was kept busy enough. Now, seated opposite each other, and looking relaxed and at ease, Mrs Gandell even smiled at Jones, and he was always prompt.

'Yes, Mrs Gandell?'

'Nothing, Jones. Just thinking.'

His voice oozed satisfaction, self-praise. 'I think we've done a very good job this morning, Mrs Gandell. Don't you.'

But already her thoughts were drawing her away from the room, nearer to the Midland Bank, and she said very quietly, 'Yes, you did an excellent job.'

'The hotel has a bright new face, Mrs Gandell.'

She nodded her approval, held on to the uncomfortable thoughts.

'I think it might be a good thing, Jones, if you went in to Davies today. Get it done with. And you had better take in a sample sheet, since I want exactly the same kind.'

'Very well,' he said.

'Then get off, Jones, get off.'

'Yes, Mrs Gandell,' and he hurried from the room.

Mr Griffith's communication still seemed to her rather abrupt.

'Surely, I can't be in the red again?'

She heard Jones coming out of the other room. He

popped his head in, saying, 'I'm off now, Mrs Gandell. Anything else you want whilst I'm in town?'

She shook her head. No. She wanted nothing. She heard him down the stairs, and a few minutes later the front door banged. He had gone. Immediately she got up and went down to her office.

' "Or phone, if you must".'

She looked at the telephone so rarely used, picked it up and dialled the bank and asked for the manager.

'Mr Griffith?'

'Speaking.'

'Oh,' and a very long oh, and then, 'Good morning,' and then waiting.

'Yes, Mrs Gandell?'

'I hope you don't mind, Mr Griffith, but this is the only morning I have free,' and would have liked to add, 'I'm so busy this week.'

'At the time stated?'

'Yes,' she said.

'Very well,' followed by a loud ahem. 'Half past ten it is, and I look forward to seeing you.'

Unlike Mr Griffith, Mrs Gandell at this moment, did not. She went to her room and changed, surveyed the Gandell countenance in the powder-misted mirror. 'I'll be glad when its over,' she thought. She picked up her umbrella in the hall, took one look upstairs, and opened the front door. She was certain of one thing. Nobody would call during her absence, and nobody would ring. Until the end of a dreadful February nobody would have the slightest interest in Cartref. She gave a little sigh as she turned the corner, and hoped for the best.

Hers was an unwanted, unasked for journey. She smiled but the once, the name Prothero coming into her mind, popping up like a fugitive. She hoped nothing would go wrong.

At the bank, Mr Griffith sat and waited for her, from time to time glancing at his watch. He cared about time, and was as punctual and precise as the clock on the wall.

Sitting back in his chair, reading *The Times,* he suddenly went to the back page, and once more went through the obituary column. This was a daily duty to do, and he ran his eye down the column. He had missed nothing. Mr Griffith often thought about an aged aunt, oceans away in Australia, whom he hadn't seen for years, and whilst she lived, he hoped. He folded up the paper, thought about Mrs Gandell. Almost a year since he had seen her. He was both knowledgeable and calculating, and there was little concerning the human condition of his clients that did not seep through the stout doors of the bank. He had a certain admiration for Mrs Gandell, a woman that refused to be beaten by the odds against her. He also thought her a somewhat foolish woman, since he had advised her on more than one occasion that her hotel would not pay. But then, she was English, from Yorkshire, and as stubborn as granite. Still, he admired her, and often enough wondered why she had ever come to the town, a complete stranger. Cartref went cheaply enough. Perhaps that was the answer.

'Its last two owners had never made it pay.' He ought to know. He thought her rather naive, since she seemed at all times optimistic, even about uncertainties. It seemed to him a long way to come in order to go through an inevitable process. The Griffith eye and ear missed nothing. On impulse he decided to receive her in a room reeking of cigar, and at once lighted one, after which he pressed the bell on his desk.

'Come in,' and his faithful ledger clerk entered and placed the Gandell account on his desk.

'Thank you, Jenkins,' and the clerk went out. He called him back.

'Yes sir?'

'How healthy?'

'Eighty-nine pounds seventeen shillings and eightpence, Mr Griffith.'

'Right.'

He looked at his watch again, at the clock on the wall.

'She's late.'

He sat back, spread legs, enjoyed his cigar. He wondered if, the previous evening, Mrs Gandell's ears had burned.

'They ought to have done,' he thought, and a thin smile came from thin lips. 'Yes indeed.'

For only last evening he had dined at The Oak with Jack Blair. Over the succulent Welsh lamb they had quietly discussed the position of a property called The Palms, a very large house of twenty rooms that had long been empty, and which, during the war, had been turned into a guest house for elderly refugees. It stood at the opposite end of the bridge, bigger than Cartref, and more threatening. The moment Mr Griffith realised that The Palms had been empty too long, he rang up a solicitor friend about it, and in a flash it was a good idea to them both. Why on earth hadn't they thought of it before. Mr Griffith's head went right back, he sent up a cloud of smoke, and idly contemplated the ceiling. 'Quick on his toes,' Griffith thought.

'Make a good hotel, Jack, get it cheap, I know the owner.'

'There's the small place at the other end of the bridge,' Mr Blair said.

'Had it in mind. The owner might sell. Having a very difficult time of it at the moment, hardly any visitors at all this winter, though the usual summer traffic. But it's a struggle for her, and she might be glad to let it go.'

'You want both?' asked Blair.

'Why not?' and he gave a vigorous nod.

'No harm in trying. Might refuse. Say she's stubborn.'

'She's from Yorkshire,' Mr Griffith said.

Mr Blair said he would certainly think about the idea.

'Good.'

'Coming in to see me this week,' Griffith said.

'Property is valuable.'

Mr Griffith had called for another half bottle of hock, lit a fresh cigar. 'You've a new typist, Jack,' he said.

Laughing, Jack said yes he had. Best he'd ever had.

'I've heard about her,' Griffith said. 'At Cartref now.'

143

'Yes.'

Miss Vaughan was on their horizon, but they would never know if her ears, too, were burning.

'If you paid her in crumbs she'd say thank you.'

'Indeed. Must come from the more desperate part of Dinbych,' said Mr Griffith, his smile suddenly expansive, a convivial evening was bound to follow. Yes he'd heard all about her, and Mrs Gandell, and the orphan of storms, Jones, and that near potty Minister at Penuel.

'If Gandell agrees to sell,' Mr Griffith said, 'she would probably go home to Yorkshire.'

'Probably. Tough for Jones.'

'She could throw him in with the fittings.'

And they both laughed.

'Rather late in the day for Thomas,' Blair said, and laughed again.

'Old man,' Mr Griffith said, and finished off the hock.

'A nice evening, Cledwyn,' said Mr Blair, rising from the table.

'And do some cogitating tonight, Jack, and give me a ring tomorrow.'

'Why not?'

'Why not indeed.'

They smiled their way out of the hotel, stood for a moment in the dark street, and after more than one convivial good night, they went their separate ways.

Griffith was still reflecting on the evening when the second knock came, and a Mr Hughes put his head in and said that Mrs Gandell had not yet arrived.

'Oh dear!' and then more hushed, 'Damned nuisance,' and he looked even more anxiously at the clock on the wall. It was at this very moment that Mrs Gandell towered her way into the bank.

'Here now, sir,' called Hughes.

Griffith got up. 'Good. Show her in,' and he went forward to meet her.

'Ah! There you are, Mrs Gandell. Nice to see you. *Do*

sit down,' offering her the large black leather chair. 'Right.'

He sat down. 'Seems ages since we met, Mrs Gandell.'

'Tell me the worst,' she said, and it surprised Griffith.

'The worst? Surely you get the quarterly statements, Mrs Gandell?'

'Of course.'

'Then what makes you think you're in the red?'

Mrs Gandell laughed. 'I'm hardly ever out of the red,' she said.

'Some mistake. Your account is here,' and he handed it to her.

'Well!' she said. 'How extraordinary, Mr Griffith.'

'You've had your black days, we know that. But nothing to worry about, and it was hardly that that I had in mind. No. Something quite different.'

She sat erect in the chair.

'Really?'

'Really,' Griffith said. And then more slowly, studying her. 'I heard the other day that The Palms, you know the house, may be started up as an hotel, Mrs Gandell. A guest house before you came here. Might make it difficult for you if that happened.'

'It might indeed, Mr Griffith, and I would not like that.'

'The position at Cartref could only be described as precarious, Mrs Gandell . . . .'

'Precarious?'

'Thought I'd let you know,' he said.

'Thank you.'

'Have you ever thought of selling?' he asked.

It astounded her, and she was half out of the chair. '*Selling*?'

'Selling,' Mr Griffith said. 'Facts are facts. Might be worth thinking about.'

Mrs Gandell thought only of Jones. 'I wouldn't sell, Mr Griffith,' she replied and sat back in the chair. 'What on earth makes you think I would?'

Mr Griffith didn't appear to know, and remained silent.

She came to the desk. 'I would never dream of selling Cartref,' she said.

'Nobody has been killed,' he said, and gave her a smile.

'But I am glad about the account. I was certain I was overdrawn, Mr Griffith. I'll never know why. There's been a lot of worry lately, and I've had the worst winter . . . .'

Mr Griffith, too, knew about the winter, but made no comment.

She took out her cheque book. 'I would like to draw twenty pounds,' she said.

'Certainly, Mrs Gandell.'

He took the cheque, called Hughes, and told him to do the usual. He saw her to the door, shook hands, said quietly, 'All the same, I should think about it.'

'I shall,' she replied, and walked out, her thoughts a ferment. Sell? Why? All very sudden. What did it mean? Perhaps there was something behind it? Totally unexpected. A surprising morning. Half way down the High Street she stopped, turned back and made her way to the back door of The Lion, and knocked.

'Oh! Well indeed! Mrs *Gan*dell!' exclaimed a surprised Mrs Hughes.

'Your husband in?'

Mrs Hughes seemed to gulp as she replied, 'Yes, he is. I'll call him. *Tegid!*'

Hughes came, was even more surprised, and Mrs Gandell pushed her way into the bar.

'Your account,' she said, and placed some notes on the counter.

'Oh! Thank you, *thank* . . . .'

'Hardly necessary,' said Mrs Gandell, and hurriedly left, leaving husband and wife staring each other out.

'*Well!*' said Sarah. 'Just think of that.'

'She's actually paid up,' Tegid said.

'Tell you something,' she said.

'What?'

'He won't come here again.'

'Who?'

'Her fancy bloody man,' Sarah said, and she rushed back to the kitchen. Tegid put the money in his pocket, and gave it a good pat.

Mrs Gandell meanwhile shot round corners and when she reached Cartref went straight to her room, and unlocked the top drawer of the bureau, and took from it the unopened letters from Mr Griffith. It was as though a flash of the sun came out of each one. 'Fancy my not opening them. I was so certain. The relief! The relief.'

She went straight to the cupboard and got herself a drink and sat down. 'I wonder why he thinks I'd sell.'

She heard Jones return. 'I'm up here, Jones.'

'Coming, Mrs Gandell.'

'Ah! You got them.'

'Yes, Mrs Gandell,' and he opened the parcel and took the sheets to her, and stood waiting whilst she examined them.

'No trouble there,' she said, handing back the sheets. 'Put them in the room.'

When he returned she told him to get himself a drink.

'Thanks, Mrs Gandell,' and she smiled, and said, 'Tut, tut.'

'Davies was very nice about it, Mrs Gandell,' and Jones sat down.

'The Davies people are always nice,' she said.

And only then did he notice she was dressed to go out.

'Going out?'

'I've been out, Jones.'

'*Have* you?'

'I went to The Lion and settled the account there.'

'Did you?' The Jones eyebrows went up. 'Oh, I am glad, Mrs Gandell.'

'I saw Mr Griffith,' she said.

It astounded Jones. He stared at her, mouth half open, and then exclaimed, 'Saw Griffith. You mean the bank? What happened?'

She nodded. 'We're all right, Jones,' she said.

'All right? You mean . . . he'll let you . . . .'

'Nothing to do with *that*, Jones. Quite another matter altogether.'

He crossed the room immediately, stood over her. 'What matter?'

'He asked me if I'd care to sell the hotel?'

'Sell? Oh no. Christ no, you're not going to sell, Mrs Gandell, you said you wouldn't, you promised . . . .'

'Here,' she said, handing him her glass, and she saw his hand shake as he took it. It shook more violently as he returned it to her, and she said irritably, 'Careful, Jones, careful.'

'Sorry, Mrs Gandell.'

'There's some talk of The Palms being turned into an hotel, Jones.'

'The Palms.'

'Yes.'

'It's falling to pieces, Mrs Gandell,' Jones said, and then he dropped his glass, seemed unaware of it as suddenly he knelt down, took her hand, said, 'You wouldn't sell, Mrs Gandell, you *wouldn't* . . . .'

'I wouldn't know what to do without you, Jones,' she said, and gave his hand a squeeze. 'If I took you back to Yorkshire, the wind would blow you back to Wales. No, Jones, I said I wouldn't sell, and I won't.'

There was no need for Jones to speak, for in his face she read the message, the familiar words. 'Wouldn't know what to do, Mrs Gandell, if you left here, left me . . . .'

'It's all *right*, Jones.'

'Iesu Grist,' he said, 'for one awful moment I thought it wasn't.'

'There's nothing else to get closer to, Jones.'

'No, Mrs Gandell,' he said, stroking again, and at last the smile.

'I am glad,' he said, 'oh, I am glad, Mrs Gandell,' and hugged her.

She pushed him away, got up and removed coat and hat. 'Come along, Jones,' she said, and everything was normal again, and he followed her out. In the kitchen he took her hand again.

'Mrs Gandell,' he said, shyly, whispering it, 'Mrs Gandell?'

'What Jones?'

He looked up at her. 'I know that sometimes you laugh at me,' he said.

She laughed now, saying, 'Well, you are sometimes funny, Jones.'

'So long as you don't laugh all the time, Mrs Gandell. That's all.'

She shook her head, gave him another smile. 'Come along, Jones.'

'Yes, Mrs Gandell.'

And in silence they began to prepare the lunch. 'It's late,' she said.

And Jones thought, 'I know now. She won't go. She really means it; and I'm not lost.'

And not for weeks had Mrs Gandell heard him singing to himself.

'Mrs Gandell?'

'What, Jones?'

'Can I go out this afternoon?'

She tossed potatoes into a pan. 'If you want to,' she said.

'Thank you.'

'Where are you going, Jones?'

'Nowhere,' Jones said, and after a pause. 'I want to think.'

9

Jones walked quickly away from the hotel, and, having turned the corner, slackened his pace, walking leisurely in the direction of the bridge. Jones talked to Jones every bit of the way.

'She's lying. She'll sell. No, she won't sell, she couldn't. Said so, swore to it, can't do without me, she knows it, she does *know* it.'

He halted a moment, took a precautionary look at the sky. 'Never even told me she was going to the bank. And last time *I* went. Even went to The Lion. Settled up with Hughes.'

To Jones it seemed a lot to happen in a single morning; on so many others nothing at all happened. He took another look at the sky. He cursed Garthmeilo. 'Almost have to cry for the sunshine.' He leaned over the bridge, watched the swirling waters go by. 'I'll close my eyes,' he said, and closed them. The waters below roared in his ears. Somewhere in the distance he seemed to hear the Lancashire shouts, saw the bright mornings, and the feet that trailed from the beach to the hall, the sand on the carpet, the sand on the stairs, the cries of a fisherman with one lone trout, and busy Mrs Gandell rushing anywhere and everywhere, and Jones handy twenty-four hours of the day. It cheered Jones up, and when finally he opened his eyes he had a feeling of giddiness, and he turned away from the bridge. He did not notice the approaching figure of a man. The first thing he saw was an advancing umbrella, and when it reached the bridge, the man beneath it. And as the figure drew nearer, he exclaimed, 'The man from The Labour.' It was.

'Hello,' Geraint said, 'and what are you doing all alone here?'

'Hello,' Jones said. 'You're a bloody long time finding us someone for Mrs Gandell. Six weeks now.'

Geraint came close, put down the umbrella.

'It's not raining.'

'It will,' Geraint said, 'any minute now.'

'Any hope?' asked Jones, 'it's nearly March.'

'That Mrs Gandell is very hard to please,' Geraint said. 'We've sent her two already.'

'The last one was terrible.'

'Gone back to Ireland,' Geraint said. 'Remember that one. Bone lazy.'

'Time's getting on,' Jones said.

Geraint guffawed. 'It's always getting on, Jones. That's the trouble, it won't stop for anybody. By the way, heard the news?'

'What news?'

'Mervyn Thomas's sister has up and left him.'

'*Left* him?'

'That's right. Walked out this morning they say, and took a train back to Hengoed where her sister is.'

'*Gone*?'

'That's it.'

'Count of the way he's going on,' Geraint said.

Jones stuttered. 'Going on, going on what, where?'

'God Almighty, Jones. Surely I don't have to give any-body like you the news. You almost seem surprised. I thought you knew it all.'

'You really mean that?'

'Some silly bitch that's come to work for Blair and Wilkins in the High Street. Lodging at your place, isn't she?'

'Poor Thomas. He thinks she might fall in love with him.'

Geraint laughed, and said, 'What a hope. Some people are plain blind,' and laughed again, and with an abrupt 'Ta ta,' rushed away leaving Jones staring after him.

'Margiad Thomas left her brother. How odd. *Very* odd. Always so strict she was, and he could see her now, in many places; the front bench at Penuel, the best tent at the Festival, the perennial collector for the African missions, the eternal enquirer after everybody's health, the brisk, healthy trot through the town, the smiles. Jones once thought of Miss Thomas in heaven, serving tea, and wearing a big newly ironed white apron.

'Poor Mr Thomas,' he said. 'So helpless. Couldn't even cut himself a slice of bread, she was so close, so attentive, the hours and the minutes spent for him, so that he would be ever free to do his duty placing the word on the tongues of all. Her only brother, her good brother.'

And Geraint's words passed in and out of Jones's ears.

'Just come by Ty Newdd now, their door wide open, nobody there, and then I saw Mervyn Thomas at the bottom of the garden, and his collar off, leaning on the wall.'

'Well indeed,' thought Jones. 'Well indeed.'

Leaving her own brother high and dry. Just like that. Awful. Such a strong family they are, skin close you might say, just getting up and going back to Hengoed. Can't believe it, really.

He thought of Thomas, he thought of his chapel, he even thought of Jones.

'Used to go there myself one time,' thought Jones, and a distant echo of the Word in his ear.

'Gone. Separated. After all those years. Perhaps for good. What'll Mervyn Thomas do? And he thought of God's runner, and the chariot flying in his head, leaning on a wall in an empty house, and no collar, and the door wide open. This *was* news. A strange world indeed. Didn't he, Jones, know, he'd only just managed to hang on to his own, clinging, clutching.

'The last time I passed their house, I looked through the window, and there Margiad Thomas was, as she always was, sitting knitting by the fire, and her brother sat opposite her, smoking his pipe, just like all was right everywhere, and nothing had ever happened. It was a message to the town, it was the flag half mast. Garthmeilo would talk its head off.'

'I came out here to think about my life,' thought Jones, 'to think about the hotel, about tomorrow, about Mrs Gandell, the place where the root lay. His life would now be altered. Perhaps Thomas will go to Hengoed, too.'

He left the bridge, took the short turn, and walked on in the direction of Ty Newdd. He wanted to see the house; the whole thing was suddenly dramatic. 'And only yesterday, I laughed at Thomas.' And there it was. The once peaceful villa. Jones stood staring at it from the opposite side of the road, the open front door, a curtain flying wildly out of an upstairs window, and no smoke from a chimney, a garden gate wide. He crossed the road, peeped over a hedge. He listened. He looked down the garden, the wall was there, but no man leaned on it. He walked slowly down the path and stopped outside the door. Looking in he saw the sitting-room door open, the study door likewise. It was as though a great wind had suddenly passed through Ty Newdd.

'Well indeed! No smoke, no fire, no sound, empty,' and he stepped into the house, stood in the hall, looked stairwards, listened again. 'Empty. Dead. I can't laugh now.'

He stepped into the sitting-room. Peeped into the study, and then he saw him. Thomas was sat with his back to Jones, and his heavy hands were clasped and lay on the desk, his head was bowed. He sat motionless. He was wearing only trousers and a vest, his hair was uncombed. He stared at the broad back.

'Weakest part of any man,' he thought. Thomas defenceless. Used to sit upright at that desk every morning, reading, studying, working it all out, asking the questions, getting the answers, planning the journeys, thinking of the souls, keeping the net tight. A course for the new day, and, after the meditation, striding the town, remembering the flock, and the names in it, forgetting none. Jones, at home with empty mornings, knew this was emptier still. A word could be warm now, any word. He moved nearer to the door. Thomas was still; Thomas had heard nothing.

'Mr Thomas.'

The words were hushed, but they made Thomas jump.

'Who is that?' he asked.

'Me,' Jones said.

'Who are you?'

'Islwyn Jones.'

Thomas turned slowly round and stared at the visitor. '*You*,' he said.

'Me,' Jones replied, and took a step into the room.

'I was just passing, Mr Thomas, and I saw a door wide open, not usual it isn't, and no smoke from a fire. And then I heard the news.'

'News?'

'Only one piece of news in the world this morning, Mr Thomas.' He noticed the uncombed hair, the slack jaw, the bloodshot eyes. 'Sorry to hear it, Mr Thomas.'

Thomas turned slowly again. 'Well?' he asked.

And Jones leaned against the door. 'I . . . .', but Thomas interrupted him, turned again, and his hands fell to his knees, and Jones watched the fingers pull hard at the cloth of his trousers.

'You're an odd lot,' Thomas said.

'I could light a fire,' Jones said, and Thomas said nothing.

'I could make you a nice cup of tea, Mr Thomas,' Jones said, and again, Thomas said nothing, but now rose, came up to Jones, stood over him, and said, magisterially, 'The last time I saw you, Jones, you were drunk.'

And for the third time Jones said quietly, 'I could light you a fire, I could make you some breakfast.'

'I'm empty,' Thomas said.

'She'll come back.'

'What's that?'

'I said your sister will come back, Mr Thomas. I shouldn't worry.'

'Jones?'

'Yes?'

'Nothing really, nothing at all,' and returned to his chair, sat, turned his back on the visitor.

'I know what being alone means,' Jones said. The sharpness surprised Jones.

'Do you indeed?'

'Yes, I *do*.'

'You can light this fire, Jones, you can do the things you want to.'

'Thank you,' replied Jones, and went straight off into the kitchen. He heard the loud slam of the Minister's study door. Head in hands, Thomas leaned across his desk.

'I am blind with trust.'

He could hear Jones in the sitting-room, suddenly caught the scent of wood smoke.

'Him,' he thought. 'Him! Of all people. Mocker! Mocker!'

Crockery sounds floated in from the kitchen, he heard the wood crackling in the grate, and then the light tap on the door.

'Mr Thomas.'

He came out, sat in his usual chair. 'Thank you, Jones.'

'Welcome,' Jones replied, and sat opposite and watched the Minister drink his tea. 'The way you are looking at me, Mr Thomas,' he said.

Cup at lip, Thomas studied him. 'Only because I know you,' he said.

'You know about me? You only said that because I know about *you*.'

'Do you really?'

'Sometimes I'm sorry, and sometimes I'm not.'

'You used to come to Penuel on Sundays, and now you go no way.'

And flatly, Jones replied, 'I go no way.'

Thomas put his cup on the hearth. 'Pity,' he said.

'Many things are a pity.'

'We walk the same bridge, Jones, but we'll never meet.'

When Thomas took up his pipe, and lighted it, Jones was glad.

'With feet in two worlds, Mr Thomas, it is sometimes difficult to stand up straight.'

'Jones?'

Jones leaned forward, eager. 'Yes?'

'You are a confusing person, Jones.'

'Sorry, Mr Thomas.'

It seemed to Jones to be the only thing to say at that moment.

'I could save you, Jones.'

'Save yourself,' said Jones.

He watched the Thomas shoulders slump, and then he rose, once again stood over Jones.

'My sister said to me last night, Mervyn Thomas, I am going away, and I will not come back.'

'Terrible.'

'Writhing in the flesh,' he thought, '*writhing*,' and he saw the Minister as a man, wide open. 'He's full of doors, you can walk in anywhere. I could go right in. *Now*.'

'Were you going to say something to me, Jones?' asked Thomas.

'I was only thinking.'

A silence fell between them.

'What will you do, Mr Thomas?' asked Jones.

And Thomas said nothing, but thought of the dream that was flat on its back.

'She has no father, and no mother, and no anchor, and no place, and no root. Think of that,' Jones said.

'What are you talking about?'

'You know what I'm talking about.'

'You came to tell me something?' asked Thomas, and Jones was somewhat astonished by the eagerness with which he asked the question.

'She shouted in her sleep one night, Mr Thomas, sometimes she leaves her light on all night. Think of that. A whole night. Once, she locked her door.' Jones paused, and then said, 'I haven't forgotten what you said to me the other day, Mr Thomas. Expect you remember. It was in the afternoon, and your eyes were glued on the front door, expecting her to come out. You said I had a common mind. I *liked* that, and I didn't mind. Never do mind very much, really, it's the split difference. You mind everything. Ah! Sometimes I even think of you, lost in your little study, lonely in a black chair, and all those lonely spiders, and the big books and the little ones. Some people are good, so you don't even have to find it out. She said you once went up to her room, and you said you didn't. Who cares, Mr Thomas. Who cares. Once, I heard her saying her prayers. Lovely. She can smile with her eyes shut. And she likes the dark, and the darker the better. Her room's *very* friendly. Sometimes I hear her coming up the stairs. Talk about fairy feet.' And Thomas's pipe suddenly fell into the hearth, and he stared at the wide grin of Jones.

'You had better go,' he said, but Jones sat tight, and very still.

'You don't want me to go at all, Mr Thomas,' he said. 'I once saw you walking down Gweneth Road, at night, and I said to myself, will those plodding feet press out the big dream? Ah! The uncertainty of *not* knowing things. Makes the lips tremble. Only yesterday I was very uncertain myself, yes indeed, but now I'm not. It's the way things go.'

'Please go,' Thomas said, and stared into the fire.

'Raining again,' Jones said, looking at the window.

Thomas rose to his feet, stood over his chair. 'Yes, *raining*, Jones.'

'What, Mr Thomas?'

And Jones was conscious of the height and weight of Thomas.

'His paunch belies the words that fall out of his mouth on Sundays.'

'Yes, Mr Thomas?' all attention.

'My sister Margiad says I'm ill.'

'You look ill.'

157

'Tell me about her,' Thomas said.

Jones sat back in his chair. 'That's why I came, Mr Thomas,' he said. 'Last night,' he thought, 'I was searching in the dictionary for a word. And where was Mr Thomas then? Lying with his head in God's lap?'

'*Tell* you about her,' Jones said.

'Please,' Thomas said. 'Though you are a man of trifles, Jones, you could be a friend.'

It left Jones speechless, and he saw the Minister return to his chair, fall heavily into it, wait.

'Can I smoke?'

'Smoke.'

'Thank you,' replied Jones, thinking of the Minister as a good man, a clever man, and here was he, Jones, actually talking to him like an equal.

'I once looked out of the window and saw her coming up the street, back from her office, and I knew she wasn't rocking with it, and wasn't thinking about it, not wanting it, not dreading it, and I said to myself it's odd, and it's not right. It should be a beautiful pain, Mr Thomas.'

'What?'

'Passion,' Jones said, '*passion.*'

'Go on.'

'Thank you. Another time I saw her walking past the chapel, night it was, one of her walks you see, does sometimes walk at night, Mr Thomas. Talk about rain *that* night. You could dance in the puddles all the way to the next county. The chapel was dark, too, and God Himself safely locked up for the night. I hurried on past her, and leaped into the next Welsh alley, and then to the road again, and passed by your little kingdom of Ty Newdd, with the light shining. The window was open, and I heard your clock ticking, and your sister and you were sitting looking at each other, and very quiet it was, 'cept for your prattling little clock.'

Thomas rose again, leaned over Jones, whispered in his ear.

'Did she get my letters, Jones?'

'*Yes.*'

'She . . . .'

'Never writes letters, Mr Thomas, never. I know. Mrs Gandell knows. When she goes into her room at night, she leaves her shadow outside. That's how it is. I think she has some knowledge of another place, Mr Thomas.'

'Another *place*?' ......

'Place,' Jones said, '*place*.'

'You're laughing at me,' Thomas said, aggressively, 'You laugh.'

'I never laugh.'

Thomas opened his mouth to reply, but nothing came out.

'I know you're in love with Miss Vaughan,' Jones said.

'I would like to speak to her.'

'Speak.'

'I am very sad, Jones.'

'I know, Mr Thomas. Once, Mrs Gandell and me were both very sad one night, bad news that day it was, very bad, just after supper time it was, and we both climbed the stairs like divers out of the sea. When we go up the doors are always locked and the curtains drawn, nothing like being careful, Mr Thomas. Yes, and then we get very close, and Mrs Gandell's bed's safe, and I'm safe. I said to her, very *very* close we were then, I said, "If that Mr Thomas that haunts this place knew how sad we were, Mrs Gandell, I wonder if he'd pray for us." And then we both did. Yes. Wished you to pray for her and me, and the hotel, and for people to come, and the rain to stop weeping, and somebody to get the sun up.'

'Sometimes, Jones, I'm afraid of being strong,' Thomas said.

'The masthead sometimes totters,' replied Jones.

'I'll have to go, Mr Thomas,' and Jones got up.

'Don't go.'

And Jones sat down again. 'A bent man,' he thought. 'Yes, a bent man.' 'I expect you got the news, Mr Thomas,' he said.

'News?'

'*News,*' said Jones.

'*What* news?'

'She's in love with a Colonel, Mr Thomas. I thought you knew that.'

'Is it true?'

'Some birds carry the seed in their mouths and never know just where to drop it,' Jones said. 'Lunching with him tomorrow, always does. Once a week.'

'I don't believe it. My sister said yesterday that . . . .'

'You don't have to believe anything, Mr Thomas, even that facts are facts.'

'Have you seen him?'

'The Colonel? Why should I? Besides he lives somewhere miles and miles along the beach. Once, one of the girls from her office followed her, but Miss Vaughan just went on and on and on, and the poor girl got tired, and she went back to her office, and told her friend Mair about it, and Mair laughed and said, "Poor dear, perhaps she's walked into the sea".'

Thomas did a quite astonishing thing, and it upset Jones. He came forward and knelt at his chair.

'Is that true?'

'That's what I heard.'

Jones never expected it, but it came, and it shocked him. 'Good God,' Thomas said, 'Good God,' and clapped hands to his face.

'I'd better go,' Jones said.

'Don't go. Not yet, Jones. Don't go.'

What hallucinatory thread is now winding and winding around his head? He closed his eyes, he could not look at this man kneeling. 'You're not well, Mr Thomas,' he said, and he helped the Minister back to his chair. 'Have you *anything* in the house?'

'There.'

Jones went to the sideboard, fixed him a nip of brandy.

'Here. I know you're sad. I'm sorry.'

He watched brandy drops trickle down the Thomas chin. It made him think of his sister at once, her face paling at the sight of it, poor Miss Thomas perhaps reeling from the smell.

'Are you all right, Mr Thomas?'

He could no longer think of him as God's man, the chariot in his head crashing, such a clever man, such a good man. 'Are you all *right*, Mr Thomas?' and felt his hand clutched, and the heaviness of it, and a kind of horror in the moment. 'He's going mad,' he thought, 'roots up, the house reeling, very soon he'll blubber, *blubber*.'

'Sorry,' Jones said, 'Sorry.'

'It is true?'

'Jones?'

'Yes?'

'I never knew you were sorry for people,' Thomas said.

'Because I never *shout*, Minister. I keep quiet, and to myself, and I never shout. Fact.'

There was a light tap on the door, but Thomas did not hear it. Jones did, and got up and went out. The girl at the door gave him a note.

'What is this?' he asked.

And the girl said, 'Miss Thomas left it with the station master, and he asked me to bring it along.'

'Thank you,' Jones said.

The girl said, 'Welcome,' and walked off down the path. Jones held the note in his hand. 'What is it?'

Thomas was slumped in the chair, his head turned to the wall.

'Mr Thomas?'

It seemed an age to Jones before the Minister said with a dropped voice, 'What is it, Jones?'

'A note, Mr Thomas. A girl just brought it from the station. From your sister it is. Here,' and he pushed it into the hand that was not clenched. He watched him slowly open it, then let it fall to the floor.

'Read it.'

'*Read* it, Mr Thomas.'

The head bowed, and Jones spread out the sheet of paper and slowly read its contents. 'Dear Mervyn, unload your nonsense, and I will come back to you, and I will look after you as always. Margiad.'

'Thank you,' Thomas said.

Jones folded up the note and lay it on the table. 'I *must* go,' and he said to Thomas, 'I *must* go now.'

'Wait.'

Jones stood, waited.

'Sit down, Jones.'

He sat.

Jones glanced at the clock, and thought it was time to go. Mrs Gandell was such a worrier about him being late.

'Yes, Mr Thomas?'

'You think I'm a fool,' Thomas said.

'I never said that.'

'What *didn't* you say?'

And Thomas was close again, his hands pressed hard on the Jones shoulders. 'My sister said that Miss Vaughan laughs at me.'

'She never laughs, Mr Thomas. Never heard her laugh once. Know why?'

'Why, Jones?'

'She laughs inside,' Jones said, and essayed the faintest smile.

'*Inside*?'

'Not for the ear. She smiles twice a day,' Jones said.

'You're not laughing, Jones?'

'Course I'm not laughing.'

It came suddenly, conspiratorially into Jones's ear.

'I nearly spoke to her last Monday. I bumped into her just outside Blair's office.'

'You should have taken her upstairs,' Jones said.

'*Taken* her upstairs?'

'Women like to be taken upstairs,' Jones said. 'Mrs

Gandell does.'

Thomas walked away, and stood staring out of the window.

'Once I was watching you stood outside Cartref, evening it was. I expect you were hoping then. And d'you know what I said to myself?'

Thomas turned away from the window, looked at Jones. 'What did you say?'

'I said to myself, if Mr Thomas really wants to talk to her, I'll charge him a pound to come in, and a shilling for every stair he climbs, and two pounds to stand outside her door. You could have listened to her dreaming. She often dreams out loud, Mr Thomas.'

'Go away,' Thomas said, and with a great weariness repeated it. '*Go* away,' and went back to his chair.

'I know why you're sending me away,' Jones said.

'Don't tell me.'

'I will. It's because I'm honest.'

He stood over Thomas, and continued. 'You're *too* good, Mr Thomas.'

Thomas said nothing, looked up at Jones.

'*And* a silly man,' thought Jones.

'Go to Miss Vaughan. *Take* Miss Vaughan. Hug her, Mr Thomas, *hug* her. One good big hug, and you'll pull her out of the clouds. Fact.' Jones turned away, made to speak again, didn't, and went straight to the door. He looked back at the Minister. And for the very first time in his life Jones felt sick, looking at this grown man, his half century beside him, locked in his dream. 'Perhaps he expects it all to come to him on a big gold tray.' He paused as he went out. 'Mr Thomas?'

Thomas looked up, but said nothing.

'And if you *do*,' Jones said, 'remember to take your collar off.'

He heard Jones go, heard the door bang, his feet heavy and grinding on the gravel path, and a sudden burst of whistling from Jones as he hurried back to the hotel. Had he remained a moment longer he would have heard Thomas say, 'God! I *am* ill,' a break in the Thomas voice, and only his sister would have got the message, and been glad and sorry at the same time.

Mrs Gandell was having tea when he got back.

'That was a long walk you had, Jones.'

Jones hung his jacket in the hall, and then sat down.

'It was,' he said, and began his tea.

'Where've you *been*, Jones?'

'Everywhere.'

Jones was hungry, and very thirsty, he wolfed tea.

'Saw the chap from The Labour, Mrs Gandell,' he said.

'Yes,' she said, expectantly.

'No luck yet. He said it's the low wages. Incidentally Dooley's gone back to St Patrick and the shamrock.'

'Will we never get anybody for that kitchen,' cried Mrs Gandell, seeing the kitchen close, suddenly hating it.

'He was quite optimistic,' Jones said.

Mrs Gandell lit her usual cigarette. She gave Jones a penetrating look. 'You've something to tell me, Jones.'

'I saw the man with the chariot in his head, Mrs Gandell.'

'Mr Thomas?'

'His sister's gone and left him.'

'Left him? How extraordinary.'

'Shame pushed her on the train at last. Gone to stay with her sister at Hengoed.'

'Oh dear! I'm sorry.'

'Sorry. You never cared anything about him. What d'you mean, sorry?'

She thought Jones would soon unwind, and she threw him a cigarette.

'You called on him?'

'Geraint Richards told me, said he'd just passed a dead house.'

'So that's where you went.'

'Silly old fool,' Jones said. 'I thought he was going to

cry. His sister's quite right, Mrs Gandell. Two men with white coats will call and collect. Things he said to me. Wanted to laugh, and I didn't, wanted to rush away, and I didn't, even wanted to be sick, but I wasn't. Asked me about the letters he pushed under her door.' Jones paused, leaned in, 'How the hell did he get in, Mrs Gandell?' Mrs Gandell didn't know.

'All the doors in the house wide open, and no fire, and the curtain flying out of the bedroom window, and him sitting in his study.'

'You went in?'

'Yes.'

'Why?'

The Jones salvo came unexpectedly. 'Because he's a man, Mrs Gandell, because he's *Welsh*, because he's a man of God, because he's mad, because he's lost, because he's afraid, because he *wants* to, because he's really *fallen* for the quiet, secret bitch upstairs.'

'Jones,' exclaimed Mrs Gandell, '*Jones*.'

'Even the cat would have been sorry for him.'

'Poor Mr Thomas,' she said.

'I told him about the man from Melin,' Jones said, and so quietly that Mrs Gandell sat up in her chair, saying, 'What's that, Jones?'

'I *told* him about the man from *Melin*.'

'The man from Melin?'

'Just like the man from Penuel,' replied Jones, and then cautiously, 'Well, nearly.'

'What on earth are you talking about, Jones?' and she grabbed him, pulled him across the table. 'Have you been drinking again?'

'Smell?'

She smelt, pushed him away again. 'Well?'

'*He* had middle years, and they sat heavy on him, just like Mr Thomas, but *she* was different . . . .'

'The what?'

'The *girl*. Fifteen and a half she was. Big difference in

years, Mrs Gandell, just think of that. Bigger sin. Know what they did?'

'Who? What?'

'They locked him in his own chapel, and flung his sheep-dog in after him, drew barbed wire all round it, nailed the door, and the leading crusader shouted through the window, "Pray, murderer". And the one that was fifteen was up in the mountains. Her father lashed the sin, Mrs Gandell.'

Mrs Gandell covered her face. 'How awful,' she said.

'Some things are. *He* prayed in the dark, and the sheep-dog howled Amen.'

'How dreadful, Jones,' said Mrs Gandell, and her hands came slowly down and rested on the table. 'Is that true?'

'Have I ever lied to you, Mrs Gandell?' He flung it at her, an ultimatum. 'Well, have I?'

She did not answer him. The cigarette burned her fingers, and she flung it away, and lit another one. 'How sad, Jones,' she said.

'Some things are. You could actually see it inside him, like a kind of crab, writhing.'

'That's enough, Jones.'

He leaned across the table, and said slowly, with a clipped utterance, 'I told Mr Thomas to get up, to shake himself. I told him to rush away and take her. Have her. Be *done* with it.'

'That's enough,' shouted Mrs Gandell, 'and I mean enough.'

But it wasn't, not for Jones, and, putting a hand over her hand, said, 'They say that the man from Melin was so *tense* that when he fell on her, he nearly pulled a nail from the cross.'

'You told Thomas that?' she said.

As though the whole world was standing in the dining-room, Jones's voice faded to a whisper, and suddenly she put a hand over his mouth. 'That's *enough*.'

'I told him to leave his collar off, Mrs Gandell. It's another dimension.'

'Disgusting.'

She got up and walked quickly out of the room.

'But real, Mrs Gandell, *real*,' Jones said, and followed her out, and up the stairs. He closed the bedroom door, and Mrs Gandell went and stood at the window for a moment, and then sat down. It was at this moment that Jones noticed the open book lying on the bedside table. He clapped hands to his head. 'Oh no,' he thought, 'not *again*,' seeing what he called the Dumas bible. '*Another* bloody chapter.' Dumas was merciless to Jones, but Mrs Gandell enjoyed him. She watched him place a tentative finger on the open book.

'You can read to me till supper time, Jones,' she said.

'*Very* well,' said Jones, and wished the Musketeers direct to hell.

10

When Miss Vaughan came swinging through the door in her red two piece, bag tight under one arm, and her red raincoat over the other, Mair knew it was Wednesday. She leaned over to Nancy, saying 'Silly old bitch,' just as Mr Blair himself was through the door.

'What was that?' Mr Blair said, tall over the low desk.

'Nothing, sir,' Mair said.

'I'm glad it is nothing, Miss Beynon,' he replied, and swept on to his office.

'Why don't you leave her alone?' asked Nancy.

'She's still a silly old bitch,' Mair said, and then got down to her typing. She rarely lifted her head above the machine until lunch time. Mair was like that; she often felt the weight of the world on her back. She was sixteen, and in two years Mr Blair would throw her through the door. Mair knew this, and didn't care. Nancy was seventeen, and would only have to wait another year. They watched Miss Vaughan hang up her coat, put away her bag, and then the bell rang, and she went off to attend to Mr Blair.

'D'you think she'll marry the Colonel?' Nancy ventured to say, and Mair barked back that she couldn't care less, and took another glance at the clock, the first of many, and at twelve-thirty promptly she would leave the office and hurry all the way home to Penrhyn Terrace. Mam would fuss about getting her lunch, and she would throw the transistor switch and sink into the chair, and listen to Tom. The world loved Tom, and so did Mair.

'Did you talk to Mr Wilkins?' Mam enquired, and Mair said, yes, she had, but it was the same message as last week and last month, the same words.

'I'll never get a raise whilst *she's* there,' Mair said, and Mam knew who *she* was, and said, 'Come long, get your lunch.'

'She works for less money than we do, Mam,' Mair said.

'You told me that.'

'I shan't stay there,' she said.

'You told me that, too,' Mam said, and served her with crisps and fish fingers.

'I want to go away, Mam.'

Mam sat, studied her. 'Don't we all?'

'You flatten everything I say,' Mair said.

'Perhaps he'll sack Miss Vaughan,' Mam said.

'Miss Vaughan might die.'

'That's an awful thing to say, dear.'

'What isn't awful,' replied Mair, and increased Tom's volume, and turned her back on her mother, announcing very directly that she was finished.

'Your father still thinks you should have stayed on at school,' Mam said.

'Aw,' exclaimed Mair, looked daggers at Mam. 'What for?'

Mair was sparing of brains, and didn't mind very much.

'What *for*?' Mam said.

And Mair wished that everyone over sixteen was stone dead.

Hammering away at her machine, Mair thought about yesterday, about Mam, and was reconciled to the fact that tomorrow would be no different. It had taken her some time to get used to Miss Vaughan. 'Good morning, Miss Vaughan,' Mair would say, and Miss Vaughan would smile, and say nothing. She was like that. Even Nancy remembered. Unlike Mair, Nancy Evans always had her lunch at the Blue Bird Cafe in the High Street. She ate fishpaste sandwiches and nibbled at digestive biscuits, and often drank three cups of tea. She thought of Miss Vaughan as being rather superior, but would never dream of conveying this to Mair, whose tongue, she thought, was already sharp enough. They heard the door open and close, and Miss Vaughan emerged from the private sanctum bearing a great sheaf of papers, which she shared with both.

'Type these letters,' she said.

They took the letters, did not look up, and did not answer her. It caused no concern at all to Miss Vaughan, since she didn't notice them very often; perhaps Mair and Nancy were there by accident. She then returned to Mr Blair's office, hovered over his desk, ready to do her duty.

'Do sit down, Miss Vaughan,' Mr Blair said, and she sat down, facing the safe, the door of which lay wide open. This safe almost burst at the seams, a rich history of people, dead and alive, town secrets, big secrets, little ones. Miss Vaughan had once been allowed to approach it, and to put away some papers, and had had a shock as she knelt there, feeling something that gave her a slight shiver, so that she turned quickly to Mr Blair, saying 'There's something not right in here, Mr Blair,' and groped, and eventually brought to view the petrified remains of a dead seagull. Mr Blair had simply said, 'H'm! Toms,' algebra to Miss Vaughan, but for him just one of the jokes of a very late office boy. And ever since, girls, and girls only, had been the order of the day. The silence of the office was broken only by the crackle of papers. Mr Blair almost lay over the desk, studying them. Miss Vaughan had taken off her spectacles, and was cleaning them when he looked up. The red-rimmed eyes surprised him, roused curiosity.

'Miss Vaughan!'

Miss Vaughan was stiff, attentive in a moment.

'Yes, Mr Blair?'

'Have you been crying, Miss Vaughan?'

She put back her spectacles, and said quietly, 'No sir, I haven't.'

'I'm glad,' he said, and bent once more to his task.

'There'll be the bank, and the post office today,' he said. '*Before* lunch.'

'Yes, Mr Blair', and Mr Blair finished with the papers, sat back in his chair.

'My wife was really disappointed the other day that you could not come to tea, Miss Vaughan.'

'I never go to tea,' Miss Vaughan replied.

And Blair faltered, fragmented the reply. 'Yes. Of course. Indeed. We understand.'

Miss Vaughan again said thank you, and then got up and went into the outer office.

'Ready?' asked Miss Vaughan.

And again the typists did not answer, and did not look up at her. Miss Vaughan was not concerned, just as though it were the thing to do. She returned to Mr Blair's room with the letters, and put them on his desk for signature.

'I could catch the twelve-thirty post with them, Mr Blair.'

A dragged 'Yes' from Mr Blair, and he paused, looked at her, his pen in the air. 'Miss Vaughan?'

'Yes, Mr Blair?'

There was a sudden softening of the Blair features, almost as if he was on the point of smiling, but Miss Vaughan seemed concerned only with his eyes. She could not recall her employer ever taking such a long look as this.

'Yes sir?' she said.

'You do not appear to me to like people very much,' said Mr Blair, and immediately he saw the Vaughan eyes close behind the spectacles.

'Some people are nice,' she replied, and opened them again.

Mr Blair resumed signing the letters, and he thought that this was the closest he had ever got to his so efficient secretary. Miss Vaughan listened to the scratching of the pen.

Still scratching, Mr Blair said, laughingly, 'I know of course that just being a person can be something of a nuisance.' Miss Vaughan said nothing, and her eye followed the moving pen.

'There,' said Mr Blair, and sat up.

She was still quiet in her chair, motionless, waiting again.

Though the question shot right out of the blue, it did not disturb Miss Vaughan.

'Miss Vaughan?'

'Yes, Mr Blair?'

'You *are* happy here?' he asked.

'I am happy here,' she said, and, knowing her, Mr Blair accepted it as final.

'I'm glad,' he said.

She gave him her first smile of the day.

'If you should change your mind, Miss Vaughan, there is still the spare room at Ty Baen.'

Miss Vaughan said she was quite content, and added, for good measure, 'Thank you, Mr Blair.'

In a moment she realised that the strict rhythm of Mr Blair's day was becoming relaxed, since he did not hand her the letters to fold up and finally seal, but now sat back in his chair, and said casually, 'A friend of mine came to see me the other day, Miss Vaughan, a very respectable woman indeed, some trouble about her brother. She was very worried about him. Some kind of emotional upset.' He paused, then offered her his usual smile. 'Apparently her brother has fallen in love with a woman in the town. I said no, since I never deal with the cases of friends.' And after another short pause, 'Get these letters away, Miss Vaughan,' and he handed her the small black briefcase that he had just taken from the bottom drawer of his desk. 'The bank first, Miss Vaughan, and then the post office.'

She folded the letters, put them in their envelopes, sealed them, and got up. She had not heard a single word of what Mr Blair had been saying, for the captain of the ship that could never sail had been talking into her ear for the past five minutes, so Miss Vaughan was worried again; she had cried in her dream about this unfortunate ship, her more unfortunate captain.

'Seventeen letters, Miss Vaughan,' said Mr Blair.

'Oh - - - yes - - that's right, Mr Blair. Thank you,' and left the office, leaving Mr Blair staring at the glass panelled door, long after she had departed.

'A strange women' he thought. Excellent at her job, never complains, always punctual, best he'd ever had – but – in personal matters, so remote, sometimes so odd, so withdrawn, so private, and had a momentary vision of Miss Vaughan wearing a large white card round her neck on which was printed in large black letters, DON'T TOUCH. He gave a quiet chuckle, and then got down to his work again.

Miss Vaughan, meanwhile, proceeded towards the bank and the post office, though, and it was unusual for her, she had slackened her pace. The ship's captain no longer whispered in her ear. It had been replaced by a sudden awesome joy that spread like light throughout her whole body, remembering as she did the words of Mr Blair's that had been so quiet and casual, so that once again she had the heightened awareness, and final knowledge that the man from Penuel was again behind her, a black funeral, ponderous and slow, his black Homburg stiff on his head, enveloped in his black overcoat. She had felt him outside the office, felt him outside Cartref, in the High Street, and smiled her secret smile. Her awesome joy increased, remembering that not once had she turned her head to look at him, and would not smile at a man that depended on them. But now, just as she came in sight of the bank, she did suddenly stop dead, and turn very slowly round and look back. He was not there. There was nobody there. She increased her pace, and stepped into the bank.

'Silly man,' she thought, as she handed in Mr Blair's income for one whole week.

'Good morning, Miss Vaughan,' the clerk said, half smiling, then suddenly grim. 'Please sit down.'

She sat down, opened her bag, examined herself in the mirror, put it back again, got up, and began pacing the room, whilst the clerk went hurriedly and accurately through the cheques before him. He then made out the receipt and called her.

'Thank you, Miss Vaughan. Good morning.'

'Good morning,' and Miss Vaughan continued her journey to the post office.

She thought of Mr Blair, pressing in his invitation to tea at his home, the offer of a room there. It occasioned no smile, inside or outside.

Having done her business with the post office, Miss Vaughan continued down the High Street, finally turning in at the Blue Bird Cafe for her usual cup of coffee. It was empty, so she rang the little bell at her table, with an idle glance at the cafe's sentry-box, and then saw the girl come from behind the blue curtains. They knew each other only by sight.

'Good morning, m'am.'

'Good morning. Coffee, please.'

The girl served her, vanished behind the curtains and left Miss Vaughan sitting by the window, slowly sipping her coffee. And again the dream was live, and again the captain was there. She thought of this, she thought hard about it. Was the boat still there, flagless, the hatches still off, the holds gaping. Was the anchor still clinging to the bottom of the sea? She put down the cup, she closed her eyes.

'He was just going to tell me about that anchor when I woke up,' thought Miss Vaughan. 'I wonder now, I wonder.' Never sailing at all, and the poor Captain on the poop, *quite* alone, poor derelict man, and staring to every point of the compass, and the wind, the *wind*. Perhaps if the weather changed all would be different, that anchor come up, the sound of it like music in the Captain's ears, the drag and the pull and the triumph of it breaking dead water, at last. And she was close to the ship now, and close to the man. And with him she slowly raised her head, looked balefully at the sky. 'Terrible,' thought Miss Vaughan. 'Terrible.' She thought of the crew, hidden, buried away in ship's holes, silent in the silence, not daring to move, wanting to, looking up, daring themselves *not* to look up. If the weather changed, if the sky cleared, if the still ship trembled, broke free of the prison. 'Poor Captain,' she thought. 'Poor man.'

She was still alone in the room, hard by the window, looking out, beyond the High Street, beyond the town. The coffee had gone cold. She had forgotten it was there, didn't see the face of the girl watching through the curtains, the eyes asking, a silence waiting to be broken.

'More coffee, ma'm,' she called, her face free of the blue surrounds, and Miss Vaughan's hand twitched violently, and the cup shook, and she looked at the girl, held the cup in the air.

'Thank you,' Miss Vaughan said, and waited.

The girl hovered and smiled, 'A little sun today,' she said.

'I see there is,' Miss Vaughan said, not seeing, but listening.

'You haven't been crying, Miss Vaughan?' and in a moment Mr Blair was *there*, looking at her, studying her, looking at her eyes, red eyes, perhaps thinking, 'Poor Miss Vaughan.'

The traffic rolled by, people passed the window, but the High Street was no longer there, and she saw only the sea, a vivid blue, a faint, thin ration of sun today for Garthmeilo. That's what the girl said to her, 'A little bit of sun today.' She hadn't noticed it, smelling only the sea, hearing the roar of it. It came through the window, washed about her table. The clock in the cafe chimed, she heard it, and was back in the world again. She got up and made for the door, and the girl came violently from behind the curtains and followed her to the door, opened it, and gave her an expensive smile. 'Good morning,' she said. 'Thank you.' The Blue Bird was glad of any business, even with half cups. Miss Vaughan said nothing and closed the door behind her, and made her way back to the offices of Blair and Wilkins.

She glanced in at the hairdressers as she passed, but the row of helmeted women seemed of little interest to her. She thought of Cartref, her room high in the sky, she thought of the closed door, and the silence. She thought of the darkness, lying in it, alone, happy. She thought of Mrs Gandell. At half past eight that very morning, and a changed atmosphere. The Gandell smile too big, and too sudden; the very attentive Jones. The woman to woman moment, a mountain of flesh bending, an arm wavering in the air, all ready to fall, sisterly, on a sisterly shoulder. The expression on the big face, the concern in the voice, the womanly whisper, the confidence.

'Have you been crying, Miss Vaughan?' Mrs Gandell said.

'Stupid woman,' she thought, expecting the same questions, the well used ones, the worn words.

'Hope you've had a good night, Miss Vaughan,' and getting the answer, and being 'so *glad*,' and the trousered shadow at her side, bending, crawling, echoing the hopes, hearing the words again. 'So glad, so glad.'

Miss Vaughan once thought of Mrs Gandell as a large child, happy, and laughing, and singing, under balloons.

'Poor Mrs Gandell. Poor Mr Jones.'

She turned the corner, suddenly stopped. People passed by and she did not see them, a voice said 'Good morning,' but she did not hear it, and then she went quickly on to the office, and knew that she was getting nearer and nearer to her day. The day she *lived*. Ten yards away she heard the rattle of the typewriters, and then entered, glanced at the girls, saw they were doing their duty, heard the quiet giggles as she passed, and held her head high in the air. There were always moments when one could make the world wait. Mr Blair accepted the bank receipt, and the stamps, without a word, and she sat down. She heard Mr Wilkins talking excitedly with a client in the next office, but it was merely a noise in the ear. Mr Blair sat well back in his chair, his face hidden behind a long parchment document. And still Miss Vaughan waited, and said nothing, and watched the clock. She opened her handbag, felt the little brown paper parcel inside it, gave a little sigh, and closed it again. Mr Blair hummed to himself as he read, and she watched the document come lower and lower, so that at any moment the Blair features would be visible. And she still thought of the day, of rainbows that could shine in even the darkest and most foreboding sky, heard the sea sing, saw the shore widen and widen, become golden and more golden.

She thought of the Colonel, tall, distinguished, twirling moustaches as he came out of the dark house, then slowly down the drive; saw the big white gate, watched him look back at the shadowed pile, then walk on and stop abruptly, and turn again. 'I hope he's not forgotten to lock his father in,' she thought, and saw him, bent at ninety, a shining pink dome, a mass of hair at the ears, and seemed to see them clearer now, winding and winding remorselessly about the bone. In which room was he locked? She wondered about that, wondering until she was tense, about the man, about the room. She heard the closing of the big white gate, and hoped that the Colonel would not be late. He had been last time; kept her waiting nearly an hour, so that she had to have her lunch quite alone, sat on a sand dune, waiting, watching, a figure over the horizon, and soundless steps all the way, and, like she, sensing the soft, flesh-like feel of the shore after the rain. Behind her spectacles Miss Vaughan's eyes were shut tight, and all she heard was the tiny crackle of disturbed papers. Mr Blair had finished his reading, and now lay the document down, looked at his watch, and said to her. 'Take any rings, Miss Vaughan, up to one'clock, and then go to lunch.'

'Yes, Mr Blair.'

He brushed lightly against her as he passed. She heard the door close. She took out the mirror, carefully studied herself, put it back in the bag, and got up, just as the two girls left their own chairs, and rushed to get their coats and hats. She passed them without a word, and went out and stood on the pavement edge. The girls followed, smiled at each other.

'There she goes,' Nancy said.

'She's still a silly old bitch,' Mair said, and made a mad rush for Penrhyn Terrace, but Nancy still stood there watching the departing figure in her red suit, and her little black hat, the red raincoat swinging on her arm. 'Poor Colonel,' she thought, as she set off for the Blue Bird Cafe. Miss Vaughan herself had left the High Street, and turned her feet in the direction of the sea. Her step lightened, her pace slackened, the breeze was strong, salt-laden, her nostrils quivered, the breeze teased at her hair. She ambled, rather than walked. Perhaps this time it would be the Colonel that had to show patience, understanding. The cold wind came upon her in waves, she glanced quickly at the sky. She looked at her watch. It was only a quarter past one. She hoped the Colonel would be there. She crossed the bridge, descended to the shore. She stood quite still, her eyes scanning the distant horizon. She closed her eyes, watched him come, felt him come. She opened them again and the shore widened, lengthened, was suddenly vast. She went on, moving inwards towards the sea, and outwards from it. Distance diminished her. She stopped again, looked slowly round. And knew that these were the best days. She was alone. Sea and shore and sky had shut off the world. Her pace increased, she swung her bag with a certain abandon, and she fixed her gaze upon a horizon that now advanced, and now receded, and thought once more of the ship, an anchor fathoms down, her captain silhouetted against a hopeless horizon. She must certainly talk to the Colonel about it. And again she hoped, willed him to be there, and went on, winding her way in and out of the dunes, then moving outwards again towards the living water. The horizon was still there, on which there was still no shadow and no man. It drew her on and on. How close she had been to man and ship, a whole night through, cradled in darkness. She had cried in her dream. And what she had drawn from sleep still lived in her head. She sat down again, opened the bag, took out the packet of sandwiches, pondered for a moment or two, then put them back again, rose, and cried in the wind. 'I wonder where he is,' and begged him to come, tall over the horizon, leaping and bounding towards her. He lifted the weight from the day, and her step lightened and slowly murdered the distances. Once she looked back by the way she had come, but only the once.

There was a man in the dunes, hidden, low in a low place, flat upon his face, his chin resting on cold hands, and he was shadowed only by the smashed keel of a rotting boat. But she did not see him.

For a full hour, after the door banged, after the outer gate had closed, after the whistling had died in the air, Mervyn Thomas had not moved, but sat stiff and hunched in the chair by the fire that Jones had lighted. His sister was not there; she was at Hengoed, deserts away, and he did not think of her. That was part of yesterday, and he was still here, in the house that was silent, locked in the room. Once he had risen, made staggering movements towards his open study door, had stopped dead on the threshold, staring within as though this room was strange, never before seen, and he a visitor there. And he looked at the book-lined shelves, the half filled wastepaper basket, the untidy desk, and the book that lay on it, and he knew that if he went in and opened it, dead words would fall from the pages that he held. He had returned to his chair, pausing a moment before he reseated himself. It, like the room, would lock him in. He sat again, his fingers kneading at the cloth of his trousers, and he accepted the rack of his own obsession. The room itself appeared to have widened, the walls heightened, a ceiling ascending. And the moment he closed his eyes there was a man in the room. He heard this man speak, laugh, heard his heavy footsteps as he paced up and down. 'Colonel? *What* Colonel?'

It made him think of Jones, and, thinking of him, he suddenly hung his head. It made him rise up abruptly to stand away from both chair and fire, made him turn towards the window, where the light lay, as he stood fully erect, staring down at himself, his hands reaching to shoulders, and then coming slowly down, all the way to his feet, as he swept away the very skin and feel of the lackey from Cartref. An emanation, a revulsion, the remnants of his nature, of his respectability crumbling, an aura of horror, and the words out of the man with a tight mouth, a mean mouth.

'Oh no,' he said, 'oh no,' into a room in which the very breath of his visitor seemed yet to hang in the air.

'Colonel who?' he cried. '*Who?*'

And shouted, 'Liar. Liar.'

He sat down, he embraced himself. 'I don't believe it.'

And Miss Vaughan was thought, and then was flesh, alone, lost, sad, moment to his moment, dream to his dream.

'I will follow her to the shore. I will speak to her. I will watch for this Colonel,' and saying it, he knew what to do. He wanted to, dreaded to, dared to. He walked straight from the room and went upstairs. In the bathroom he washed and shaved, changed his clothes, put on a clean collar, then sat down at his dressing-table, and carefully combed his hair. He looked at his reflection in the mirror. Was he too good? Too bad? Was he a fool? The obsession rose, raced again. Again he brushed at the grey-black hair, a moment of uncertainty, an indeterminateness that slowed both hand and brush, which finally fell from his hand. He closed his eyes, refused to look at the man in the mirror. Hesitant rising, he was again hesitant at the door. Then he walked out and hurried down to the hall. He went into the garden, walked its length and back again, then once more returned, to stand by the tree where yesterday he had seen his sister stand, her head turned from the house that was home. He looked up at it now, and it seemed to him as though he had never lived in it, his study, and his life there had never been. As he retreated his steps he thought he heard his own father speaking to him.

'You will always be the man in the corner, Mervyn. Always.'

He took his overcoat and hat from the stand and put them on, walked to the door and opened it, gave a final glance at the sitting-room fire, and left the house. There was a bite to the wind, and he drew up the collar of his coat, made more secure the Homburg on his head, thrust hands deep into pockets, and, head down, hurried away from house, and street, and road, and there was the bridge to be crossed. The wind struck sharper still, and he smelt the sea before he saw it. And the figure on the sands walked up and down. When he reached the middle of the bridge he paused to clutch at the rail, looked both right and left. The waters smashed below, he looked up, he looked round again. A day for closed doors and windows, and coals to fires. A strange day to meet a Colonel. He continued his journey. Would she be there? Wouldn't she? And *him*, that man, would he, too, be there? Thomas wondered, Thomas hoped. Words moved upon his tongue, but never left it, and unspoken they yet propelled him forward, and as he moved he thought of 'the Colonel' and he dreaded him, and he hated him. He wished he was absent, *gone*, dead. Suddenly his feet touched shore, and he began to walk slowly along, and after a while sat himself down. Silence arched the world. He felt in his pocket for a pipe, but it wasn't there, and he said under his breath, 'Damn!'

'Every Wednesday,' they said, 'Every Wednesday.'

He lay flat upon the sand, he stiffened, and then relaxed. He turned over on his back, stared up at the sky. When he shut his eyes it was suddenly dark, and darker again, and darker than that. The wind was cold, it clawed at his hair. He got up again and went on.

'I am walking out of my life,' he thought. 'I am walking out of my life,' he said. Sea against wish, shore against hope. There was no one there. He thought he saw a distant figure approaching, and he went down on his knees, hid behind tufts of grass. Was it her? Wasn't it? It came

nearer and nearer, but it was only a low-flying bird, master-
ing the wind, the only living thing, supreme in the emptiness. He went on with bowed head. Once, and how vividly
he remembered it, he had stolen into the hotel, crept up the
stairs, stood outside her door, listened. And he had spoken to
her, and she had even answered back. The scene was vivid
in his mind, then, quite suddenly, a man named Jones had
blotted it out. Jones was *there*. He couldn't remember where
Mrs Gandell was, and it had never mattered. And he was
hidden at the top of the stairs, and Jones was clearly visible
at the bottom. Thomas sat down and listened.

'Come down, man of God.'

And he had not answered.

'I'll swear I locked this door before I went out,' he
heard Jones say, noticing a thickened speech.

'He's drunk,' Thomas said to Thomas. 'He's drunk.'

He remembered the loud creak on the stair.

'I said come down, man of God,' and Thomas came
slowly down.

'You must have come through the wall, Minister. I'll
swear I left this door locked.'

Jones leaned against the wall, but now came out, pressed
hands to his hips, watched Thomas descend, got close to
him, looked up into the florid features. Jones smiled.

'Good evening, Minister. It is very late. I hope your
sister is not too well. And what is the answer?'

Thomas felt awkward, felt humiliated, was disgusted at
the smile, too close, and Jones hiccuped in his face as soon
as he reached the bottom stair.

'Not *too* close, Mr Jones. The world knows that you
have just left The Lion.'

'Ah,' Jones said, 'I *see*. No collar, Mr Thomas. You
could be anybody without it, and even less than that. I expect you left it hanging in the best bedroom at Ty Newdd.
Well. Well.' Jones rocked on his heels, swayed a little. 'A
splendid sight,' he said. 'You seem to have forgotten a for-
mer message, Minister, and Mrs Gandell will be displeased,'

and he leaned closer still to Thomas. Thomas pushed him rudely away. 'You smell, Jones,' he said. Jones pinned him against the wall. 'There's no hurry,' he said.

'Get out of my way.'

'I only wish I could, Mr Thomas.'

Thomas gripped him, pushed harder. '*Get-out* of . . . .'

Jones grinned. 'Was she flat on her back, Minister. Staring upwards. Yes, you do look ordinary now. Embrace the fact.'

'I said get out of my way.'

'Was her bed full of grace and angels, Minister? Did she cry out in her dream?'

Thomas had forced him back, so that Jones found himself pinned to the wall.

'I am stronger than the man with the chariot in his head,' he said, and laughed, and then was free, so that instantly Thomas was aware of the hand at his shoulder, and a hand under his chin.

'Ah,' Jones said, slobbered a little, if *only* you could have opened that little door in her head. *I* know. Mrs Gandell knows. She doesn't even read your mad letters. But if only that little door had opened. *What* a strange and precarious joy might have popped out.' He felt Jones's breath in his face, and pushed harder still, but Jones held him tight, and still smiled in his face.

'I can't get out of your way, Mr Thomas,' he said. 'I can't. God! You are a damned fool, that is, for a clever man. Miss Vaughan loves Miss Vaughan. I love *me*. What's wrong with it?'

Jones pressed, and Thomas pressed, but there was no movement. He saw the Jones teeth, heard the words coming through.

'*She* laughs. I laugh. Mrs Gandell laughs. We all laugh,' and after a slight pause, 'Garthmeilo laughs.'

'Liar.'

Jones banged the Thomas head against the wall.

'Here! Who are you calling a liar?'

'When common little men get drunk,' Thomas was

saying, and then he felt Jones's hand pressing hard on his mouth.

'Ever notice how she holds her head in the air, Minister. Do-you-know-*what*? Sometimes she sings to herself in bed. Heard her. Hear everything in this house,' he said, and followed it up with a low titter. He put his mouth to the Thomas ear, saying, 'Mrs Gandell said it *wasn't* my night off, but I knew that it *was*. So I took it. Plastered her with gin first. Cheers her up. She's probably as flat as a dead trout now,' and Jones laughed again.

'I don't want to knock you down, Jones,' Thomas said.

It made Jones grin all over again.

'Some of Miss Vaughan's friends live on the stairs, Minister. Just think of that.'

Thomas heaved again. 'Damn you,' he said.

'Ah, naughty man of God,' said Jones, and whispered, and was close again. 'Have you ever heard her saying her prayers, man of God? I have. But only the once. And after that I expect she justs waits.'

He felt his shoulders gripped, he felt himself being pushed slowly backwards. 'You've a snake's tongue,' Thomas said, still pushing.

'No you don't,' and the strength of Jones surprised the now imprisoned man. 'Tell you something,' he said, 'before you go, before I push. I once went into her room, though I left my shadow outside, yours would drown the wall, Minister, but she wasn't there. No indeed. Once saw her reading a book, once saw her actually *smiling*. I think she has a special knowledge of other dimensions. Hee hee.'

Thomas got a hand free, and quite astonished Jones by striking him across the mouth.

'You're a twisted creature, Jones.'

'*And* I've a very common mind, man of God. Remember. You told me that the other day. Course you remember. It was in wind-blown Jubilee Street. *I* didn't mind. Never did mind many things. In a minute you can go, Mr Thomas, back to your study and your leather chair, and those lonely spiders, and the big books, and the little ones. Ah! There are some people that are so good that you never have to find out about it.' Jones gave a sudden belch, then continued, 'My bloody head's just beginning to clear, Mr Thomas. If only a real bishop could see you now,' and Jones laughed, and went on laughing. He dropped his voice, he went on, wet lips, wet words. 'I myself never climb stairs unless doors and windows are locked behind me. I like to have curtains drawn very *close*, and Mrs Gandell's bed is always so *safe*, and hers is, which is the same thing of course. Funny. I was just thinking of your sister, Mr Thomas, and all those socks she knits for you. Waiting up for you, is she? When you get home, you can if you like, say a teeny weeny little prayer for me. Will tomorrow be like today? I expect so, and your big feet still pressing on that big dream. Just think of the uncertainty as you mutter the words, as your lips tremble. Almost every night, my head is buried in a silly bloody book. Mrs Gandell's very romantic, Mr Thomas. But I expect yours is buried in God's lap. Once, I even got buried in a dictionary. Think of that, me, Jones. Wish you'd pray for us both, Minister, *and* the hotel, *and* the rain to stop weeping, *and* somebody to give the trout seekers a real big push in Welsh directions. Ah! That would be just lovely.' They were clear of the wall, they struggled on the carpet, and upstairs Mrs Gandell snored.

'Once, she shouted in her sleep, once she left her light on a whole night. But always locks her door. Isn't that odd,' said Jones. 'Yesterday morning we watched you coming, Mrs Gandell and me, saw through a top window, and I said to her, "Just look at that, Mrs Gandell. The way he walks, I said. Mr Thomas on sentry by the door, waiting, and inside he is rocking with passion, and thinking about her, and wanting her, and dreading her at the same time. Just like a nice pain." You *are* a bloody fool.'

Thomas felt himself grabbed by his coat collar, pushed towards the door, the Jones words falling into his ears.

'There's the door. And the world is *outside*, Minister, and anybody staggering down London Street can dance in the rain if he wants to. Expect you'll have to pass Penuel on your way home. 'Spect you'll see that God Almighty is locked up safe for the night. After that you cross another little street, down another road, and there you are, and you'll see the light shining at Ty Newdd. I shouldn't think your sister knits socks at midnight. Some women in fairy tales used to, so I understand. Sometimes I think there's a little madness about everything. Don't you?'

He opened wide the door, but Thomas appeared rooted where he stood.

'*Come* along,' he said, but Thomas had not moved.

'I said you could *go*, Minister,' and he glanced upstairs. 'Expect she's still asleep, slugged by Gordon's, or was it Booths?'

Thomas seemed to fall forward, suddenly clutched at the door.

'You're not ill?' said Jones, and pulled him free. 'Drop your hands, man of God, and turn your toes southwards. Go *away*, close this door after you, and shut fast your own when you get home, and nail yourself to the floor, and *pray*. Tell your sister that I was asking after her. I *do* know good people from bad, in spite of your authority, and the Word on your tongue that seems so final. Good *night*,' and he shot Thomas into the darkness.

And Thomas lay in it, and pushed his cold hands into the sleeves of his coat, and stirred his body slightly, and peeped from behind the grasses, and wondered if she would come. Suddenly he exclaimed into the wind, 'Ugh! *Ugh!*' as though Jones were still there, but Jones had vanished. He came to his knees, scanned the shore. There was nothing there. He got up, paced up and down, rubbed his hands, and seemed to hear Jones say, 'You are a bloody fool.' Then he lay down again, drew in his head under the sheltering collar. He waited for the woman. He watched for the man. And he did not feel the cold.

The town felt it, and it turned its back on wind and sea.
There was a woman on the shore, walking, walking where?
Let her walk. The town was sense, and it leaned to its fires,
but there was nonsense on the shore, under the sky, close to
the sea, that this day was grey, foam-tossed. Cartref had
closed its doors and windows. March was strangling February. Even Mrs Gandell realised this, sat at her table in the
dining-room, the eternal cigarette dangling from her mouth,
and she watched for the door that would open. And where
on earth was that man Jones? Gone over an hour now,
with a basket on his arm. An altogether new duty for him,
and it still surprised. She wished he would come. She hoped
that a hot breakfast wrapped in a white napkin, and a
flask of hot coffee would sustain a minister on a very strange
morning.

'I still can't believe his sister would go off like that,' she
thought, even as she got a glimpse of Thomas outside her
hotel, sneaking about, hovering, waiting and watching and
listening for the sharp steps on the stones.

'Is that you, Jones?'

It was. He came in, put the basket down on the table,
and sat down.

'No good, Mrs Gandell.'

'No good?'

'Wasn't there.'

'Wasn't *there*?'

'I *said* it, Mrs Gandell,' and he watched her unwrap the
napkin, put the breakfast on the table, remove an un-
touched flask.

'Perhaps he's still in bed,' she said. 'Did you knock hard?'

'Front door locked, but I managed to get in at the back,

and I called and called. No answer. Looked in his sitting-room, his study, went upstairs, called again. Looked in the rooms. No answer. Not there, Mrs Gandell. Empty.'

'I've seen him once or twice at the Blue Bird place,' she said, recalling two fugitive visits into Garthmeilo.

'Perhaps,' Jones said. 'I'll bring it in, Mrs Gandell.'

'Do.'

And Jones went off to the kitchen for the lunch. Over breakfast they had discussed the minister.

'He's not used to being on his own,' Mrs Gandell said.

'And now he's finding out,' Jones replied.

'Whatever you may think of him, something should be done.'

But Jones didn't hear, remembering at that moment only a new Miss Vaughan.

'Did you see *her* this morning, Mrs Gandell?'

'Of course I saw her. I thought she looked rather nice in that new get up of hers.'

'Think she'd been crying. Watched her clean her specs.'

'You told me she never cried, Jones, that she couldn't.'

'Red eyed this morning. Had a bad dream, I expect. Not all dreams have sugar in them, Mrs Gandell,' and when she did not reply, gripped her arm. 'Well, *have* they?'

'If it pleases you, Jones. *No.*'

During lunch he astonished Mrs Gandell by clapping hands, shouting 'Hurrah', as children do, and he smiled across at her. 'February's *gone*, Mrs Gandell. Actually, truly gone.'

'I did notice. Have you seen March,' she said, and directed the Jones glance to the window.

Like Jones, she too, had forgotten Thomas, was thinking of tomorrow, her new arrivals, Mr Prothero and friend. They would bring with them a new colour, especially to clash against a perpetual grey. Already she could hear the Prothero chortles, the peals of laughter; she made play with his jovial nature, listened to the coarse joke, accepted a fake heartiness, and more important, drew the coin from the Prothero pocket.

'Think of it, Jones. Tomorrow. Two of them.'

Jones's voice lacked enthusiasm, he said that he was aware of the fact.

'I don't much like him, Mrs Gandell,' he said. 'Call him plastic John. Talks too much, too loudly. Don't you think so?'

She didn't think so, and said so in no uncertain manner.

'One *shilling*, Mrs Gandell, for services rendered,' and she noted the disgust in his voice. '*One* shilling. Think of that.'

'No need to think about it at all, Jones, since you accepted it.'

'Tegid Hughes said that if you gave him a kick in the backside, six more backsides would grow in its place at once,' Jones said. She wasn't listening, and she wasn't going to laugh. It didn't seem to matter.

'Clear away, Jones.'

'Yes, Mrs Gandell.'

'Here,' and she flung him a cigarette.

'Thanks.'

'I'd a girl here this morning,' Mrs Gandell said. 'From The Labour.'

'Oh! You never told me,' and Jones put the tray on the sideboard and went to the table. 'What girl?'

'I'm telling you now. I liked her, she's seventeen, and looks useful. She's Welsh.'

'Indeed.'

He picked up the tray and went out.

'What a relief,' thought Jones, seeing himself free at last from all that washing up, a new girl doing her duty. Nearly time, too.

Mrs Gandell sat up, smoked her cigarette, and thought of tomorrow. When he came back she had gone. He thought he heard her calling.

'Calling, Mrs Gandell?'

'I was calling.'

Jones stood on the stairs. 'If she's lying, if she sells over my head, I'll cut her throat,' and he went on up, found her sitting on the bed.

'There ought to be a fire here, Mrs Gandell. And those curtains should be drawn. And the damned window still open,' and he rushed across and closed it. Jones loved being shut in.

'Tell me about the bank,' he said.

'I told you.'

He stood over her, and said, 'Then tell me again, Mrs Gandell.'

'I thought I was in the red, and I wasn't. That's all, Jones.'

'I don't quite understand you,' he said.

'Look in the cupboard.'

'Well indeed,' said Jones looking in, smiling. 'When did this happen?'

'This morning.'

'Having one?'

'Not now.'

'Mind if I have one?'

'Have one.'

'Thanks,' he said, and helped himself to a gin, after which he sat down beside her. 'I can't believe it,' he said.

'I can.'

He finished his drink, got up and went to the small chest of drawers, knelt down, and opened the bottom drawer.

'Anything wrong, Jones?'

His reply was immediate, and quite sharp. 'Not yet,' he said, and put the glass down, and dived into the drawer.

'Let the bitch wait,' he thought; the ground still seemed uncertain under the Jones feet.

'Tell me about The Palms.'

'The *Palms*?'

'What *about* it?'

'Is something wrong, Jones?'

'I don't quite know. Is there?'

She lay back on the bed. 'Aren't you coming?' she asked.

He turned on his knees, gave her a long penetrating look.

'I'm thinking,' he said.

'Your thoughts'll be much warmer over here,' she said.

'Shut up.'

She sat up at once. Was he trying to start a row?

'Have you got one of your awful little moods again?' she asked.

He did not reply, got up, and went to the bed. He leaned down.

'Mrs Gandell?'

'Mrs Gandell is listening, Jones,' she said, and smiled up at him.

'I want you to do something for me,' Jones said.

'I'm waiting,' she said.

'Im not thinking about what's on *top* of your mind, Mrs Gandell, but what's underneath it,' and his hands pressed on her shoulders.

'What the *hell* are you talking about?'

'Are you going to sell this place?'

'I am not going to sell this place.'

'You said that once before. Remember?'

'I'm saying it again. *Now.*'

She grabbed his hand, gave a pull. 'Come along Jones,' she said.

He pulled himself clear. 'Wait,' he said, and returned to the chest of drawers, from which he took out a large book bound in brown leather. He closed the drawer. Mrs Gandell sat up, leaned on an elbow.

'What *is* all this, Jones?'

He lowered the book to within an inch of her head.

'See this?'

'What is it, Jones?'

'*Read* it.'

'Bible,' she read.

'That's right, Mrs Gandell,' and she felt the flat of the

book on her head. 'I didn't realise you could read so well,' he said, acidly. 'I want you to put your hand on this book, and I want you to swear on it.'

'Swear on a bible?'

'Swear on it that you won't sell Cartref over my head.' He lowered the book in front of her. 'Now,' he said.

'Really, Jones,' and she pushed both him and book away. '*Really*. Don't you believe me?' She laughed, and Jones didn't.

'Don't laugh,' he said.

'Swear? On this?'

'On that,' he said, took her hand, and placed it on the book. 'Swear, Mrs Gandell, swear. One has to be so careful with people, *always*.' And her hand was flat upon the book. 'I swear,' she said.

'Again.'

'I *swear*.'

'I swear that I will not sell this hotel. Go on. *Say* it.'

'I will not sell Cartref, and I swear on it,' Mrs Gandell said.

'Thank you, thank you, Mrs Gandell,' and he bent down and kissed her. He returned the book to the drawer, then went to the grate and put a match to the fire, after which he drew the curtains. 'There's real cosy for you,' he said, spreading his arms wide. He stood over her again. 'Have you ever been lost, Mrs Gandell?'

'We could both get lost now,' she said.

'I'll never leave you now, Mrs Gandell,' he said. 'Never.' He began to undress, and she switched out the light.

Hands pushed into his coat sleeves, Thomas crouched in the sand. He was on his knees, watching, waiting. From the rear he looked absurd, from the front, earnest and hopeful, sad and bewildered. Again he saw a bird flying his way, but it was only Miss Vaughan walking straight towards him, and then he saw her.

'It's her,' he said, out of a dry mouth. 'It's Miss Vaughan,' and his head vanished behind a tuft of grass. 'I'll speak to her.' And he watched her come nearer and nearer. Seeing her more clearly, he was struck by her movements. She seemed to swing towards him, seemed at times to float her way along. She would suddenly stop, then bound forward. Thomas flattened himself in the sand. She walked past him, then stopped again. He saw her sit down, open her bag, and take out a packet of sandwiches. He watched her open it, begin to eat.

'Lunch? *Lunch*? I don't understand.'

She was in profile now, and he watched her remove her glasses. He wondered at what she was staring. 'How tense she looks.' She ate her sandwiches, she seemed in no hurry.

'What is *happen*ing?'

She turned her head from time to time, searched up and down the shore, then turned again, and stared out to sea.

He saw her roll up the sheet of paper and fling it into the wind.

'I've never been so close to her, never,' and he raised his head a little. 'What will she do?'

He looked beyond her, expecting the man. 'I'll soon know.'

It was at this moment that she got up and walked towards the sea. Thomas knelt again, followed her every step.

'Where is she *going*?'

He saw her dart forward, hold out both hands, heard her cry into the wind.

'Colonel. There you are,' she cried, stopped dead, ran forward again.

And the words came with the wind, into Thomas's ears.

'I thought you were never coming,' she said, and threw herself forward.

'Good God!' and the Thomas hand went quickly to the Thomas mouth, as if to smother the words that had startled him. Miss Vaughan shook hands with the air. 'How are you, Colonel?' She waved again, cried aloud, 'At last. You're here, Colonel.' Thomas came slowly to his feet. He watched a fresh movement of hands as she cried, 'Down Suki, *down*,' and patted the head of the dog that did not bark. More words drifted back to him, and they were crystal clear.

'I hope your father is safe, Colonel,' Miss Vaughan said, and linked arms with him, and together they walked up and down the shore. 'Safe,' and the leap in the voice. 'I'm glad.' Thomas felt himself drawn further and further away from the dunes. And he watched her pat the dog again, turn her head sharply, look up.

'I thought you'd *never* come,' she cried. 'I waited and waited, and waited, and I looked at the sea. It's so beautiful today. I've a little shell in my room, Colonel. I often hear the sea roar. Wonderful. Have you ever heard it roar close to your ear?'

'Oh no,' exclaimed Thomas, 'Oh *no*.'

He stood erect, he stiffened, he wanted to shout, 'Miss Vaughan! Miss Vaughan!' and his lips trembled, and nothing came out.

As she came bounding towards him, Thomas fell flat on his face.

'Come along, Colonel,' she cried, and pulled him after her.

She was so close, he thought she might hear him breathing. He saw her sit down again, close by, very close.

'So *glad* you came today. I wanted to tell you about the ship. You remember the ship, don't you, and its anchor clinging to the very bottom of the sea. You said you *knew* all about it, you were going to tell me about the captain, but you didn't.' She laughed then, and shouted, 'I shall tell *you*. Most extraordinary, the crew aboard and never sailing at all. Think of that, Colonel.'

'Oh God,' Thomas said, and did not realise he had spoken. She turned her head from him, and her conversation became more animated. 'The long, long time I've thought about things, many things. And *how* the weather has changed, so suddenly. And this wind, Colonel,' and she flung her hat into it, let the wind play with her hair. 'The sand is so beautiful. I'd like to dance on it,' she said. Low in his throat, Thomas muttered, 'Colonel. There *is* no Colonel.' 'Let's walk a little,' Miss Vaughan said, and she was off again, and Thomas was staring, and went on staring.

'Poor . . . no, no no . . . .'

He watched her pat the air, he watched her take the Colonel's hand in her hand.

'*Down* Suki, down.'

'D'you remember a day when I walked all the way to your house? And you weren't there. I felt cold in a moment, and I knocked, and knocked, and knocked,' and Thomas saw her stare straight at the Colonel.

'There was no answer. You weren't even *there*. God alone knows where your father was. I remember crying to myself, "Gone, gone where?" ' Her voice was hushed. 'And then I went closer, I looked through a front window. Quiet it was then. And I saw the big room. I saw your father standing in a corner, and a hand to his ear, listening. It was *so* silent. I once heard my father sing to my mother, "Take him to that far corner, and lay him down," and I remember following him to the corner, but only the once.'

Thomas watched Miss Vaughan grab the air.

'I once was followed a very long way by a man, Colonel, but I never looked round, and he went on his way, and then I forgot him.' She turned violently left, still clinging on to the Colonel's arm, gave a little run, and stopped again.

When Thomas saw her arms widen, he knew that she had embraced him. Her voice grew louder, more anxious, more persistent.

'I remember a day when I nearly *died*. Think of that, Colonel. Died.'

'So that is the Colonel,' thought Thomas, his voice sepulchral, choking. 'Out of the air, out of the sea.'

'God help you' Thomas said. 'I still love you.'

'There's a ship now,' she cried.

'Poor creature,' he said, and shut his eyes.

'The wind,' she cried, 'I love the wind,' and he saw her waltz the Colonel round and round, and then back to the dunes. She sat, she punctuated her words with a finger stabbing the air.

'The first time I ever saw the world, Colonel, was out of a tiny window at Cae Mawr. Do you know Cae Mawr? Oh, you do. Fancy that. You've *been* there, and she clapped hands. 'It makes me think of my father, made me think that I'm forty-five today. Imagine that, Colonel. As you grow up, my father said, the roads will get longer, and the walls higher. Age is for tumbling, he said. I think of that. The sea was very far away then, *very* far. I thought you'd *never* come today, Colonel. I said to myself, "Perhaps he is not being careful with his father, perhaps he hasn't locked the door." If you had *not* come, I would have gone straight back to my room. I have a key. I would have locked the door, put out the light. Hidden. My father was sometimes wise, and sometimes, very good indeed with the words of Christ. He was also of the law, and very very careful of the law.'

'To what am I listening,' thought Thomas. 'And at what am I looking?'

Thomas gripped the grass, hugged the sand, then suddenly he could no longer see her, she was not there, and it had grown quite dark, and darker again, and darker than that.

'My sister did not say that I was blind,' Thomas said.

'Suki! *Suki!*'

And Thomas opened his eyes, and she was there again, close.

'Miss Vaughan,' he thought. 'Miss Vaughan,' he said.

She was so near, and yet so far, so strange, so lost.

'Miss Vaughan,' Thomas said.

Miss Vaughan was suddenly bolder still, her hands clasped tightly and lying on her knees. She looked neither right nor left.

'Miss Vaughan,' Thomas said, and rose slowly out of the ground. 'Miss Vaughan.'

And she saw him, and he was real.

Thomas got a vision of red, an explosion from the dune, and then she was running, madly, wildly along the shore.

'Miss Vaughan! Miss Vaughan,' and he was running after.

'Poor creature,' he said, 'Poor Miss Vaughan. I still love her,' and ran, and ran, and ran.

There she was, flying before his very eyes, that had been so near and yet so far.

And he ran on and on.

He saw her make wide, and more widening circles across the sand, he saw her fall.

'Oh God,' he said, running still.

He stood a moment, exhausted. When he fell, when he knew he was falling, he shouted at the top of his voice. 'Miss Vaughan! Miss Vaughan,' and watched her rise, watched her move further and further, watched the sky, and the light beginning to go.

'If I could catch her, hold her, speak to her,' Thomas said, and words thrust him forward again, and he ran on. His overcoat flew open, flapped like a sail, and his eye was fast upon the figure that sometimes ran, and sometimes stopped; sometimes dallied, and sometimes turned round and looked back, where, in the distance she could yet see a bridge, and behind her the shore, and more shore, and yet more shore. She did not see Thomas stumble again, fall to the ground, lie there; she did not hear him call her name. 'Miss Vaughan,' he shouted, came to his knees, cupped hands, cried again, 'Miss *Vaughan*!' his spirit riding behind this endeavour of flesh and bone, then rising, and shouting again. 'Wait! Wait! Miss *Vaughan*!' and the words lost, the name lost, torn to shreds in the wind.

'I must. I must.'

Suddenly she was walking, and not running, he wondered if she would stop, if she would turn again. If only she turned, came back, came his way.

'I knew it in the chapel that night. I know it now.' He stopped to button an overcoat that he did not realise was holding him back, and he felt for the hat that was no longer there. And he went on, blindly, determinedly, as though this was the journey that was final. One did not turn back, but went on, and on again. He sat down, bowed his head, and he prayed quietly for the figure that was now moving out towards the sea.

'Miss Vaughan! Miss Vaughan!' shouting again, stumbling on. Once he thought he saw the sky and the sea meet, once stopped abruptly to listen, and heard the laughter following after. 'The sea, the sea,' he shouted, then fell flat on his back. He felt lost in this vastness, and emptiness, in the silence that seemed total.

'I can't go on,' he said, and went on, and there on the horizon was the figure, still moving, further and further away. Or was it just another bird? The sand pulled, the wind held, and he went on, dragging his feet after him, his hands now pawing air itself, and wondered when she would stop, when he would stop. He clapped hands to his head.

'Oh God! Perhaps I am mad.'

And went on nearer and nearer to where sea and shore would meet.

'I cannot go on,' he cried, 'I cannot go *on*,' and went on, the roads of his life behind him, the world reduced to a moment.

'I'm coming,' he shouted, 'I'm *coming*.'

And then he saw her stood quite still, almost as though she were waiting for him to come. And Thomas cried in his mind, 'Wait. Wait.' He stopped again, he closed his eyes. For a moment he seemed to sense that he was falling again, falling down, and down, and down again, and lower than that, and his hands reached out to grasp, to hold.

'Where am I?'

His finger tips touched his eyelids, he was afraid to open his eyes.

'Where is she?'

She was there. Motionless, her back turned on him, she was still waiting. He thought of her silent life, he was in the chapel again, under the hooded light, he felt her eyes upon him. What was she thinking? *Now.* Miss Vaughan was drowned in the wind, and the sea was lapping at her feet. Thomas stopped again. How small she was, and still as still.

'If only she knew, if only she understood.' And Thomas moved again, hoped again. He saw her close, so close, and he had spoken to her, calling her name. And she had leaped away. The look, the violent movement still shocked and frightened him. He wanted to cry her name now, wanted to shout 'Wait, wait!' and dared not. His heart leapt when she turned slowly round. Was she looking at him? Was she looking beyond him, was she actually waiting for him to come?

Almost without realising it he was calling her name, he was shouting at the top of his voice. 'Wait, I'm coming, Miss Vaughan.'

Miss Vaughan moved nearer to the sea, and Thomas fell flat on his face. And then he knew that he could not move. 'Oh *Christ*,' Thomas said, hearing it and knew that he had said it, his mouth touching sand, the word falling, the word dying in it, his arms stretched out before him. And then he hammered with clenched fists, 'What shall I do with the moment?'

As he tried to rise, as he rose, as he cried out again. 'Wait! Wait!' But she did not hear him, and, unlike Thomas, seemed to know what to do with her own moment as she walked further and further away, and never again looked at that staggering figure in black that came on, lurching this way and that, and never heard the words from his mouth that the wind fragmented, that the sea's roar drowned.

'My *God!* She's walking into the sea,' he cried, and dragged himself to his feet, and lunged, and fell again, and again rose, and the shout frantic. 'Wait! Wait!'

He watched, he hoped again, he was anguished, he fell again. He dragged himself into a kneeling position, he leaned on his elbows, he cupped hands again, and cried at the top of his voice. 'Miss Vaughan! Miss Vaughan. Wait! *Please*. Wait. *Wait.*'

He saw her raise her hands in the air, as she went on, further and further in, as the sea pulled, as the moment died in him, as he opened his mouth to speak and could not, as he fell flat on his face again, and lay there, inert, a black heap, and the light going fast. There was a word on his tongue, and it wouldn't move, he knew the word that was closest to him, but it froze there, the lips mouthed air. He heard nothing, and felt nothing, and saw nothing. After a while he fell asleep.

When he woke it was fully dark, and the sea soundless. There was no wind. There seemed no sky.

'Where am I?'

He did not know. With the flat of his hands he forced himself into a sitting position, he turned his head from right to left. There was nothing. No sound, and no world, and no moment.

'Where am I?' and he seemed scarcely to realise that he

was now standing on his own feet, buried in darkness, and nothing to listen to save the sound of his own breathing.

'I *am* lost. Oh God! I am lost,' and his arms stretched, and his hands searched about for a hold, on something, on anything, and there was nothing. He moved, and did not realise that he was moving, he made to kneel again, to rest, and did not, and walked on, back by the way he had come, and again he cried into the emptiness, 'Where am I?' and the echo of the words came back to him, and he did not hear them. And he walked on, and there was still nothing. He put a hand to his head, but there was no hat. He ran his fingers down the length of his body, felt the buttons of his overcoat. Running fingers through his hair, he felt the sand in it. He fell to his knees, clasped hands, he prayed against nothing. And then he was walking again, through the desert, through the darkness. He did not realise that the bridge was there, that he was standing on it, clutching at its rail, feeling its cold bite, and the air about him itself frozen. If the air was struck it might ring like a bell. He stood there, blind, aimless, wondering which way he should go. Back? Forward? Then for the first time he was aware of wild water below the bridge, smashing in the darkness, and at once he felt the plunge and leap of the river under him. He turned away and went slowly on. He saw a light that danced suddenly, and then was gone. He saw another and another, and then he stopped. 'Where am I?'

The house staring at him, the door, the windows. When his hand found the white gate he gave a violent jerk. He listened. There was nothing. Just the house, and the rooms in it, and the door that he had left open. Like a thief he crept down the path towards his own home, felt the door, the pull of it as it moved inwards, and stumbled, and went in, and stood quite still, holding it. There was no light, and no sound, and no person. There was no warmth, and there was no meaning. His hand touched banister, his feet stairs. He clung to it, listening. He waited. Nothing. And he went upstairs. He did not notice an open sitting-room door, nor the door to that room that had once so fully contained him, and then he reached the top. Clinging to the banister, he said in a low, shaky voice, 'There is nothing,' and immediately descended the stairs. He groped his way to the sitting-room, and there was no fire. From one emptiness to another, and he stared at that which was his study, and walked into it and sat down. 'I am mad,' Thomas said, 'I am mad,' and he switched on the light, and there before him were the days and the hours and the moments, and the root and the bone, and he touched things on his desk, and held them in his hand, and put them down again. He touched the Book. He pushed it slowly away from him, and he heard the thud as it fell to the floor. He opened the top drawer of his desk, and searched about, and then he switched out the light. He lay his head flat upon the desk, and closed his eyes. The lips parted, as though he would speak, but only air came out. When the words came, they were as loud and clear as bells, and smashed into the silence.

'Let no man deceive himself. If any man among you seemeth to be wise, let him become a fool, that he may be wise,' Thomas said, and after the wreck of words, was silent. It was cold in the room.

Miss Margiad Thomas plays Patience at Hengoed, and from time to time glances dubiously at the letter lying on the table, and wonders whether she should post it tomorrow, to wish her brother cleansed.

'She knew when she was happy, and Thomas didn't,' Jones said. 'She asked for nothing, and wanted nothing, and she never got anything because she never wanted it.'

But Mrs Gandell said nothing.

At Dolgoch cottage Mrs Humphreys jumped in her chair, and exclaimed, 'What on earth was that, Emyr?'

'Sounds like somebody back firing,' Mr Humphreys said, and he got up and closed the window.

Miss Vaughan has had lunch with the Colonel, but no one will ask her to tea.